THE LAST RIGHTS

ELLIOTT LIGHT

Black Rose Writing | Texas

ISBN: 978-1-68513-679-6
LIBRARY OF CONGRESS CONTROL NUMBER: 2025939736
PUBLISHED BY BLACK ROSE WRITING
www.blackrosewriting.com

Printed in the United States of America
Suggested Retail Price (SRP) $19.95

The Last Rights is printed in Minion Pro

*As a planet-friendly publisher, Black Rose Writing does its best to eliminate unnecessary waste to reduce paper usage and energy costs, while never compromising the reading experience. As a result, the final word count vs. page count may not meet common expectations.

Cover art designed by Anita Dugan-Moore of Cyber-Bytz, www.cyber-bytz.com
Author photo by John F. Morgan, John Morgan Photography, www.jfmorgan.com

Praise for
The Last Rights

"Elliott Light manages to show us several sides of a controversial issue from the aspect of legal rights and basic human rights. Gritty, revealing, and unashamedly truthful, *The Last Rights* takes us on an emotional rollercoaster, giving us glimpses of the dark underbelly of our justice system. Be prepared to put your politics aside and leave your blinders at home."
–Gin Coleman, Author & Storyteller

"*The Last Rights* gripped me from start to finish, with each new layer more gripping than the last. This is a unique, immersive, and brilliantly written book that I couldn't put down, even after multiple reads."
–Sana Abuleil, author, *Letters to the Person I Was*

"*The Last Rights* examines the intersection of politics and women's health and wellness. The subject is not only timely but also starkly illustrative of women's lack of agency in today's American society. Elliott deftly taps into the female psyche and draws his characters with insight and compassion."
–Dr. Sandy Stahl, Assistant Provost for Student Life; Senior Lecturer in Women's and Gender Studies (Ret.)

"Intelligently written and drawn on contemporary themes, I was instantly involved. When the last page was turned, I was in awe at the brilliance communicated in the pages. This simple and entertaining story, a must read, is a metaphor for so much that is wrong in the world today, and in doing so offers up where hope lives. I loved this one."
–Paulette Mahurin, author

"*The Last Rights* checks all the boxes relating to the country's current abortion and unethical leadership crises. A superbly conceived and executed plot with believable characters and a convincingly thorough treatment of law and the (often corrupt) justice system. A gripping and engaging must
–read!"
–Dr. Charles J. Rieger

ACKNOWLEDGEMENTS

My life has been made better by people who have supported my compulsion to write and tell stories. I owe you all more than a thank you, but that will have to suffice.

To Sonya, my life partner, who reads all my drafts with a critical eye, I marvel at your patience.

To Chuck Rieger for eagerly reading drafts and providing detailed commentary.

To Sandy Stahl for advocating tirelessly for everything I write—to her friends, book clubs, bookstores, and, apparently, everyone she meets.

To Sana Abuleil for not only editing my first draft but for her encouragement to pursue the publication of my book.

I am blessed.

The LAST RIGHTS

CHAPTER ONE

Dreaming of your fifteen minutes of fame is harmless—until it comes true. At thirty-five, I've had three encounters with fame—specifically, one fame and two infamies—and don't desire another.

If you google Ashley Corbin and tennis, you'll find articles about how at sixteen, I was a tennis phenom. I was good and getting better. However, the competition I was up against wasn't challenging, which made it hard to be certain. Then, I won a state tournament and came in fourth in a national tournament, earning me the title "up and coming," the girl with the "magical forehand and serve." That was my first "fifteen-minute-moment," and I reveled in it.

But in that hit list, you'll also come across articles describing how at nineteen my budding tennis career ended suddenly when a pickup truck T-boned my car. I spent a few weeks in a coma. When I finally recovered—if *recovered* is even the right word—my shoulder was functional but would never survive the rigors of competitive tennis. The magic was gone. The story was sad and tragic, but not newsworthy. The media forgot about me and so did the tennis community.

That was my second fifteen-minute-moment, although one could quibble about whether it actually lasted that long.

Thankfully, the more personal details of my condition remained private. No one had asked where I was going before the collision or why I was assigned a bed in the prenatal wing of the hospital. The full scope of my tragedy was there for discovery. I was simply not famous enough for anyone to look.

And more recently, if you were to search my name without the word "tennis," you would find yourself flooded with stories about the rape trial I lost and how I ended up at the center of the most horrendous murder case in state history. I might consider this my third fifteen-minute moment, but my daughter, Harper, and I are still living with the consequences of that day. While I'm not the primary focus of these stories, my involvement and lack of memory of the events spawned lots of speculation about what "really" happened.

Life isn't just about the memorable bits, but what happens between them. If, twelve years ago, you had been in Freeman's Gate, you might have heard whispers about my arrival with a three-year-old, purchasing a house with cash, and living without a husband or any evidence of marriage. Naturally, the townsfolk raised questions about the baby, her father, and the purchase of my house, among others, and all were fodder for gossip. Questions without answers are ripe for narratives that explain and titillate. The residents of Freeman's Gate excelled at this form of creative storytelling.

My biographical information on the State Attorney's website isn't as entertaining:

"Ashley Corbin received her BA in history from Piedmont State College and a juris doctor degree from the Harlan School of Law. She practiced both civil and criminal law at a private law firm before joining the state attorney's office."

What the "about" paragraph doesn't reveal is after I passed the bar, I took a paralegal job at a law firm in Freeman's Gate because, according to the founding partner, it was the best a single mother could expect with a "second-rate" law degree. Over time, I became exceptional at reviewing and editing briefs. The firm rewarded me by assigning me cases none of the other associates wanted. After being overlooked for a much-earned promotion to counsel, I received an offer from the state attorney's office for a prosecutorial position and accepted it.

Freeman's Gate is my home and, until recently, a place where I felt safe. It is here I raised Harper, taught tennis at the local rec center, and volunteered at a local animal shelter that cares for stray and homeless cats. This was my happy place, a place where, despite hardships, I was blessed to live.

Sadly, my feelings for the village have changed, but it would be unfair to say the change was solely because of the murders. Freeman's Gate was not immune to the socio-political forces dividing communities across the country. Like other residents, I did my best to ignore the realities in plain sight. By the time I realized how these forces had transformed the attitudes and values of the community, it was too late.

The murders that now define my life were the culmination of the vitriol that had infected the discourse in this once-quiet town, but not the cause of it. How I became embroiled in these events is difficult to explain. Looking back, so much had to go right (or wrong, depending on your perspective) for me to be a player in the two shootings that left five dead. I've replayed the "what-if" game in my mind repeatedly. If I hadn't gone to the fraternity party, if I hadn't gotten pregnant, if I hadn't been involved in a traffic accident, if I hadn't gone to law school—lots of ifs—I might not have become involved in the series of events that led to the killings. But if compelled to pinpoint the most decisive factor, it would be my assignment to prosecute Sheila Fanning's rape case against Daniel Lockhart.

The state attorney, Martin Hudson, gave the Sheila Fanning rape case to me last August. Rape cases are uncommon in small towns, not because rape doesn't happen in them but because only one in four victims of sexual assault file a complaint. In small communities, where people know each other, the filing rate is much lower.

Martin chose me to lead the prosecution because, in his words, "You are the best people-person we have." Humbly, I was the best litigator, but not the best choice for the case.

While it was obvious I was a single mother, it wasn't obvious or known how I ended up that way. Martin had no way of knowing Sheila and I shared the experience of being forcefully violated and the silent rage that flowed from it. On an emotional level, I wanted Daniel Lockhart to be tried, convicted, and executed in some deliciously painful way. But after reviewing the circumstances of her assault, I voiced my opposition to bringing the case to trial. I believed the case was going to be difficult to win, not because of the facts, but because of the way a jury would perceive the victim and the accused.

Daniel, the accused, was a pillar of the community, a history teacher, and a community volunteer. Whether it was a food drive, flood cleanup, or the construction of a playground, Daniel was there. Sheila, the victim, was a cleaning woman, a member of the invisible inhabitants of our town who were replaceable and, therefore, valueless.

Sheila would pay a price for seeking justice. A trial would force her to relive the attack in graphic detail before a jury of strangers, to endure the insinuation that she was lying or perhaps an opportunist hoping to compel Daniel to pay to drop the charges. The verdict would depend on which of them the jury believes. Would Daniel's peers really take away his freedom based on the word of a stranger? The answer was no, *unless* the evidence of rape was overwhelming. To me, it was a close call—too close.

Normally, the prosecutor in charge has discretion over litigating a complaint, but in this case, Martin, Sheila, and, to my surprise, the state's attorney general, Carl Hinton, overruled me. Hinton's involvement in the matter was unusual, and I should have recognized it as a sign the trial of Daniel Lockhart was special. In the heat of the argument over whether to pursue the case, the sign went unnoticed.

Harper, my fifteen-year-old daughter, was also keen on my prosecuting Sheila's case. Surprisingly, Harper had met Sheila a few times after school and knew she worked as a cleaner at the school and was studying law. They weren't friends, but friendly. If Sheila claimed Daniel Lockhart raped her, then it must be true. Case closed. Harper is a champion of the underdog, just one of many reasons I admire her.

My hero status as the defender of Sheila Fanning extended beyond my daughter. Apparently, Harper was receiving positive social media posts because her mother was "cool, pretty, and really smart." Harper shared little of this chatter with me, but occasionally, I'd see a post on her computer that included the word "awesome." Once I saw the word "hot" and it made me laugh.

The trial was scheduled eight months later, which I found surprising given the speed of securing a trial date. Even more surprising, the expedited scheduling was at the behest of the defendant, Daniel Lockhart, and with the blessing of the attorney general. Again, another sign something about this case was off, and like the other signs, it, too, went unappreciated.

Harper was at the age where the concept of rape was both titillating and frightening, while also provoking a desire for retaliation and accountability. Her assessment of Daniel Lockhart, who taught her history at her high school, was that he was guilty and should go to prison for a long time. I tried to explain that the Constitution guaranteed everyone a right to due process and a fair trial and that the state could only incarcerate Daniel if I convinced a jury he was guilty beyond a reasonable doubt. This prompted a discussion over what reasonable doubt meant and how it sounded like a man guilty of rape could still go free if his defense attorney was clever enough to confuse a jury.

I didn't know it then, but Harper's cynical prescience was about to manifest itself in the tragedy that awaited Sheila Fanning—a tragedy in which I would play the leading role.

CHAPTER TWO

The lead-up to a trial is both exciting and nerve-wracking. It is akin to opening night at a play in which the lines are all ad-libbed and where the characters—the witnesses, the defense counsel, and the judge—could say anything. As the prosecutor, I had only a few nanoseconds to respond to whatever was said. A good objection, one the judge sustained, or a probing question that rattled a defense witness, was satisfying. Months of preparation culminated in a single performance. No encores.

A lawyer I once worked with offered advice that I've never forgotten: "The job of legal counsel isn't to win the case. Rather, a competent lawyer must make sure the truth survives the trial." While I wasn't keen on trying the case, I was determined to ensure the truth of what happened to Sheila Fanning wouldn't get lost amid legal maneuvers and irrelevancies thrown out by the defense.

Trials have a personality of their own. Some are dramatic. Some are boring. Some are just tedious. The trial of Daniel Lockhart was something else entirely. I sensed it when I entered the courtroom the day the proceedings started and each day thereafter.

Defendants are often nervous, which can manifest as being giddy or somber and withdrawn. But not Daniel. Before the judge entered and gaveled the court to order, he stood at the defense table looking nonchalant, confident, and even cheerful. He joked with his defense counsel, Phillip Dunlevy, and smiled at well-wishers who approached him.

What caught my attention was how often he locked eyes on the jury. Jurors are usually intimidated by a courtroom. Most look at their hands, the judge, an attorney interrogating a witness, or the victim, but not at the accused. Maybe it was because Daniel was so animated that he attracted undue attention, or maybe I was imagining things, but two jurors—one male and one female—seemed to smile at him.

Daniel's demeanor wasn't the only surprise. When the judge strolled in from a side door behind the bench, I was stunned that the one in the robe wasn't Judge Virginia Garret, a fair and by-the-book jurist, but Judge Hugh Tawney, a man who had a reputation for allowing witnesses to spew out prejudicial testimony and for wrangling with prosecutors whenever the opportunity arose.

As Judge Tawney took his seat and gaveled the court into session, an eerie silence descended on the courtroom. He panned the room, pompously enjoying being the center of attention, then pointed the gavel at me. "All right, Miss Corbin, call your first witness."

My strategy was simple. Use the police to establish the circumstances of the assault. Follow the police testimony with Sheila's testimony about how Daniel overpowered and raped her. Finally, use the evidence gathered at the hospital to support the version of events offered by Sheila and the police.

I first questioned Joyce Little, the policewoman called to the hospital in response to a complaint of sexual battery. She testified she spoke with the victim about the attack, where it occurred, and how the encounter with her assailant unfolded. Joyce confirmed Sheila sought medical treatment immediately after the attack and that her version of the attack had remained consistent over multiple interviews with detectives.

When I asked if Sheila could describe her assailant, Officer Little scoffed. "She didn't have to. I mean, she identified him as Daniel Lockhart."

The statement stirred a buzz in the courtroom that the judge quickly extinguished with a rap of his gavel and a demand for quiet.

Daniel's attorney declined to cross-examine Officer Little, and she stepped down.

I went through the same process with a detective who investigated the crime scene and found the condition of the classroom—overturned desks, spilled cleaning supplies—consistent with a struggle.

The last police witness I called was the arresting officer. The most telling part of his testimony was that Daniel Lockhart initially denied knowing Sheila Fanning. When he was told that she identified him by his watch and a tattoo on his hand, he changed his story to say that he had heard a noise in the classroom and found that Sheila had fallen and simply tried to help her up. When the officer reminded him they were going to take a saliva sample for DNA analysis, he claimed that she'd come on to him and he impulsively had sex with her.

My case against Daniel Lockhart had gone according to the script I'd prepared in my head. The jury heard that the police found Sheila credible and that Daniel, the victim, was a liar and had offered three contradictory statements about his connection to the victim. Despite a tedious cross-examination of the arresting officer painted Daniel as untrustworthy and most likely guilty.

I questioned Sheila carefully. The jury didn't need a graphic depiction of forced sexual intercourse. Rather, they needed to see Sheila as a vulnerable, sympathetic victim whose life mattered. In her own voice, she told the jury that at the time of the assault, she was working as a cleaning woman to pay her tuition at law school and that she was almost ready to graduate. She was excited about her future. After the rape, everything changed. She lost her job, missed her exams, and watched as her marriage fell apart.

When I turned my questioning to the assault, the courtroom fell silent. The jury was laser-focused on Sheila. She answered my questions forcefully, without hesitating. No, she didn't have a prior relationship with Daniel, but had seen him a few times at school. Yes, she may have spoken to him, but only to say hello or to acknowledge something he said to her. She mostly focused on her work and listened to music through earbuds.

When I asked her to tell the court what happened on the night of the assault, she turned to the defense table and stared at Daniel. "I was cleaning my classroom when Mr. Lockhart entered the room. He grabbed me from behind, covered my mouth with his hand, and ripped off my clothes. I tried to fight back, but he hit me, threw me to the floor, and forced himself inside me. While he was on top of me, his hand gripped my throat, and I was afraid he was going to kill me. That's when I saw his watch and the little tattoo on his hand. I knew who he was. I knew who was raping me."

To prove rape, I needed to show the intercourse between Daniel and Sheila was involuntary and procured by force. Because there were no eyewitnesses, the evidence to support a finding of rape was circumstantial. The jury would have to infer from this evidence that the sexual intercourse was rape and not consensual. My task was to convince the jury that the inference of rape was so powerful that it was correct beyond a reasonable doubt. The defense only needed to offer other interpretations of the same facts to create sufficient doubt in the minds of the jurors that they'd refuse to convict.

My expert witness was Priscilla Tremble, an emergency nurse and an expert in sexual assault trauma. Priscilla described the bruises on Sheila's neck, wrists, and arms, as well as a mark below Sheila's left eye. A ripped fingernail left an open and raw wound on her hand. What looked like a bite mark was visible on her left shoulder. The photos were clear and convincing. As the images were displayed on a large screen, I heard women on the jury gasp.

The first day of the trial ended before the defense could cross-examine her. The truth, as I knew it, had survived. The testimony of the state's witnesses pleased me and, while tempering my optimism, I told Sheila so.

As is my custom, I spent the evening sequestered in my bedroom, reviewing the case file and editing my closing argument. Harper knew that other than having dinner together, I was to be left alone. No television, no text messages, no distractions. The protocol was still in force in the morning when I made breakfast before sending her off to school.

Day two of the trial began with Priscilla back on the stand, facing Daniel Lockhart's attorney, Phillip Dunlevy. Phillip was a middle-aged attorney with a slightly stooped back and a voice that sometimes quivered. In his opening statement the previous day, he denied Daniel raped Sheila or assaulted her. Instead, he asserted Sheila had flirted with Daniel and lured him into a sexual encounter he simply couldn't resist. According to his version of the encounter, Sheila was the aggressor and her injuries resulted from passion, lust, and exuberance and not any criminal conduct by Daniel Lockhart. He may have used poor judgment, but he didn't rape her. He couldn't. He was a teacher, a man known for his community service. He was and is a good person.

He finished his statement by admonishing the jurors not to believe everything they heard from the prosecution. "You will be told that the so-called facts in this case lead to only one conclusion. But all we really know is that these two adults had aggressive sex in a classroom at the high school where Daniel has taught for a decade. This is a classic she-said he-said case. No witnesses. No way to know for sure what happened. Why Mrs. Fanning is accusing Mr. Lockhart of rape is anybody's guess."

He paused briefly and took a deep breath, then exhaled slowly while shaking his head. "Mr. Lockhart doesn't have to prove he's innocent. He doesn't have to testify because the state has the obligation to convince you beyond a reasonable doubt that he raped Sheila Fanning. The state can't because he didn't. Thank you."

Phillip's job was to attack the inferences that my witnesses had teased from the circumstantial evidence. He didn't have to prove anything. He just had to make the jury wonder if the evidence was susceptible to more than one interpretation. He hadn't cross-examined the police officers or Sheila aggressively, leaving me to wonder what his strategy was.

He began his cross-examination of Priscilla by asking if rough sex could have produced the same injuries. I expected the question; I even thought it might have been imprudent to ask because it reinforced the idea the sexual encounter had been forceful.

Phillip was an actor, a man who played in a community theater as a hobby. Mostly, he played the part of the older father figure with a silky, deep voice and a Midwest drawl. Whether that was his natural voice or just an affectation, I didn't know. Regardless, it was effective. He always received an ovation from the audience, even if his part, or the play, didn't justify it. Now the beloved actor with the silky voice was defending a beloved teacher, a pillar of the community, a man who couldn't hurt anyone, much less commit rape. If a member of the Walton family thought Daniel innocent, how could he not be?

Phillip knew drama and how to create it. He nodded when Priscilla answered affirmatively, then stood for a moment and seemed to ponder the answer. Sometimes I wondered whether he'd dozed off or lost focus. But then, he asked the question that I hadn't.

"When sex is forced, do you expect to find other injuries? For example, vaginal tearing?"

At the mention of the "v" word, the courtroom went silent. The jurors fidgeted, their discomfort at the anatomical reference apparent. Coming from the lips of the gentle grandpa figure, the vocalization even stunned me.

"Injury to the vagina and labia are common in rape cases, but are not always present," said Priscilla.

Phillip returned to the defense table and sorted through a stack of papers. "Just one moment, your honor."

I'm sure the jurors were worried that he might present photographic evidence of the aforementioned injuries and body parts. Instead, he pulled papers from the stack and presented them to Priscilla.

"This is a copy of your report. It's marked State's Exhibit 35. Now, can you tell the jury if you found that Miss Fanning suffered any vaginal injuries?"

"She did not," Priscilla said.

For a moment, Phillip seemed captured by his own thoughts, then asked, "When a married couple engages in lovemaking, what prevents these injuries from occurring?"

I was struggling to articulate an objection, finally rising to object on the grounds of relevance.

The judge seemed equally eager to change the subject. "Let's get to the point, Mr. Dunlevy, or move on."

"So, as to married couples?"

"Cooperative sex," said Priscilla, "is preceded by arousal. Arousal produces lubrication in the female, which facilitates penetration by the penis."

Some members of the jury looked at their hands. Others inhaled audibly, while a few coughed. For the jury, the testimony had brought back the discomfort from long-forgotten sex education classes. For me, the testimony was infuriating. The state law protects victims of sexual assault from questions that have little probative value and are intended to shame the victim. But before I could object, the next question had already made it past Dunlevy's lips.

"So, perhaps Mrs. Fanning was aroused and cooperative, which could explain the lack of injury?"

I was on my feet, objecting to the question and demanding to approach the bench, but I was too late. Whatever the judge did, short of a mistrial, couldn't take the words out of the jurors' heads. He motioned Dunlevy and me forward, but the look on his face made clear he wasn't sympathetic to whatever objection I was planning on making.

"First, counselor, lower your voice and kill the attitude. Before you start, let me make clear the question doesn't fall within the protections of the Rape Shield law. You opened the door to the question of injuries when you brought in an expert to testify to the injuries Miss Fanning suffered. Any inference from the fact there was no vaginal tearing is up to the jury. Now, step back, and see if you can undo the damage on redirect."

Phillip wasn't done. He positioned himself in front of the witness. "May I call you Priscilla?"

"Fine," she said.

"Is it fair to say a person who suffers a tearing injury isn't likely to experience pleasure?"

"Yes."

"So, someone who felt pleasure most likely wouldn't be in any serious pain?"

I stood, but the judge cut me off. "Let's move on, Mr. Dunlevy."

"That's all, your honor."

Priscilla asserted on redirect that arousal and even pleasure were not unusual in rape victims because these were physiological responses—responses that a victim couldn't control. Sadly, some victims believed that because their bodies had responded naturally to the sexual assault, the rape was their fault.

Priscilla had said the right things, but the defense had presented the jury with an alternative explanation for why there was no vaginal tearing: the sex was consensual. Even without a scintilla of evidence, the defense had successfully introduced an element of doubt into the allegation that Daniel raped Sheila. It didn't help matters that when Priscilla stepped off the stand, Sheila's husband, Quinton, bolted from the courtroom.

I used my closing argument to remind the jury the evidence of rape was overwhelming and that the arguments about arousal were irrelevant. I implored them to apply common sense. Why would a young woman choose to have sex in a classroom? The answer was she wouldn't. What did she have to gain by seducing a teacher? The answer was nothing. The fact remained that Sheila, a young woman studying law and working a menial job to pay for her education, had no interest in Daniel Lockhart, nothing to gain and everything to lose. I thought I saw some women nodding, but as I turned to return to my seat, the feeling I had lost control of the trial overwhelmed me. Perhaps I never had it.

Phillip Dunlevy delivered a passionate closing, attacking the evidence, Sheila's motives, and the law that allowed women to ruin the reputation of a stalwart of the community with no corroborating evidence.

The judge sent the jury to deliberate. With the case in their hands, all I could do was hope they would see through the attempt of the defense to blame Sheila for being raped and find Daniel guilty as charged.

CHAPTER THREE

I was gathering my papers when a tall woman with dark eyebrows set against a tan face and framed by a crop of short silver hair approached me.

"Helena Davis." She offered me her hand, a gesture that reinforced her masculine features. "I'm Sheila's mother."

I felt her eyes on me, her intense gaze seeming to measure me.

"Mrs. Davis, I'm sorry we haven't chatted."

"It's Miss, but please call me Helena. I know you're busy, but I wanted to thank you for standing up for Sheila."

"No need. I'd add it's my job, but that would make it sound impersonal. I have a lot of respect for Sheila and the courage it took to bring charges against Daniel Lockhart. I only hope that I convinced the jury of his guilt."

I was eager to go to my office and decompress, maybe play a few hands of solitaire or look at funny cat videos. But my response to her gratitude hadn't placated her, and she continued to hover over me.

"I'd like your honest opinion about the trial and Sheila's odds of winning."

Helena spoke directly and without emotion. I liked that.

"I can't offer you a lot of insights because juries are unpredictable, but I can offer you a bad cup of coffee and as much of my time as you'd like."

Helena accepted the offer with a quick smile and a nod of her head.

We found a table at the courthouse café. I cleaned it as best I could with napkins, and we sat down. Several moments later, a bored young man arrived with a dirty towel. I waved him off, ordered two coffees, and smiled at Helena.

"What would you like to know?"

Helena curled her lip, then studied me. "Sheila says you're a straight shooter. I know you opposed filing a complaint, but that's not what I want to discuss. You were looking at the jury and the defendant, so I watched them as well. I had the impression that ten of the twelve jurors were listening and taking notes. Two weren't paying attention to the testimony at all. When they were engaged, they were looking at the defendant. Is that what you saw?"

I have spent hours with victims and loved-ones waiting for verdicts. Most victims just wanted reassurance the trial went as expected. Helena was the exception. She wasn't a passive participant. She'd spent her time reading the courtroom like an attorney. And she was right.

"The behavior of the two jurors is worrisome. Whether it means anything, time will tell. We need all twelve to vote to convict. The defense only needs one to hang the jury. If that happens, I don't think the state will want a retrial. We have one shot to win the case."

The coffee arrived. I could tell from the aroma that wafted from the cups that the coffee had been on the warming plate too long. Before I could complain, the server left, presumably to wipe his dirty cleaning rag over a few more tables.

"The judge didn't like you. I don't think he likes women much."

I laughed. "You were paying attention. That's his reputation. But most of the jurors are women. If they think he was unfair to me, they may be sympathetic to Sheila."

"I've been observing you as well. Something is worrying you. Care to share?"

I took a sip of coffee, set the mug on its saucer, and pushed it away.

"Quinton. Leaving the courtroom like that…I don't know."

Helena nodded. "Quinn and Sheila were high school sweethearts. His big dream was to build beautiful homes that were also functional and energy efficient. He had cause to think that way. He was as skilled a builder as you'll find. He was big and strong and liked to get his hands dirty. When it came to construction, he had an eye for detail. They were married, and he earned money building houses for a large contractor. He was a rising star, but he wanted to be the man, the boss. The problem is, Quinton has no business sense."

"Did he treat Sheila like he was the boss?"

"Not the way you think. When other men looked at her, Quinn took it as a compliment, like guys do when someone admires their truck. But if he thought Sheila was returning the look, or even smiling, he'd sulk, like she'd hurt his feelings. He was a man-child. I tried to tell her, but she wouldn't hear it."

"So, how is their relationship now?"

"Quinn used all their savings to buy a parcel of land where he planned to build energy-efficient homes with open floor plans and lots of glass. He could talk your ear off about geothermal heating and solar heat capture. But he didn't read the contract and didn't ask the right questions. Only after the closing did he realize that the land didn't perk, so he couldn't install septic systems, and that the well water was foul to two hundred feet. The note was called in, but he couldn't pay the interest. Quinn wouldn't take a job because that would admit defeat. He faced failure like the coward he was by drinking himself numb and leaving Sheila to support them both. He's a loser. Now, they're fighting constantly. That marriage is over, but she refuses to see it."

"I'm sorry…"

"He bolts from the trial and *she* goes home to console *him*." Helena closed her eyes and grimaced. "She's consoling *him*." Helena leaned over the table. "I swore I saw Mr. Lockhart's lawyer nod to Quinton just before he left the courtroom. It seemed planned. Theatrical. But maybe I'm just imagining things."

I fiddled with a spoon. "I'm not a pessimistic person. I believe in the rule of law, which sounds corny, but it anchors me. Lawyers play games in courtrooms all the time. Most don't work. The judge instructs the jury to consider the evidence in the record and apply it to the law. It shouldn't matter what Quinn thinks, or that he left."

"Spoken like a lawyer. So, if that's the case, why do you look troubled?"

I took a deep breath and massaged my temples. "Because sometimes it matters. When Quinton walked out, I thought the jury looked shocked. Of course, the reason he left is open to interpretation. Did he leave because he believed Daniel raped Sheila or because he believed she was enjoying a tryst with him? The jury may not have an answer, but the questions alone create doubt. That's what the defense wants. I tried to keep the jury focused on the facts, but I don't know if I succeeded."

My phone buzzed. The jury had reached a verdict. I didn't tell Helena, but this wasn't good news.

CHAPTER FOUR

Thirty minutes later, Sheila and I were sitting at the prosecutor's table. The judge hadn't arrived and everyone was talking. I didn't look at Sheila, but focused my attention on her accused rapist, Daniel Lockhart. As a rule, I remain indifferent to the accused. Some are despicable, while others are tragic figures who have become victims in their own right.

My job was to argue the facts and the law objectively. For whatever reason, Daniel was different. Watching him converse jovially with his lawyer was galling.

"Ashley?"

I wasn't sure I'd heard my name, but then Sheila patted my hand.

"Mom said you discussed the case with her. I hope you know I appreciate your efforts, no matter what happens."

No matter what happens. That sounded ominous. But I was already preparing for the worst. In my thoughts, I saw the imminent future, and it made me cringe: Judge Tawney would ask the forewoman of the jury to read the verdict, Daniel and his lawyer, Phillip Dunlevy, would high-five, and the process of second-guessing me would begin. The media would question why the state attorney assigned Ashley Corbin, a thirty-five-year-old prosecutor with no experience in sexual assault cases, to try a major felony case. A faceless press corps would shout an assortment of stupid questions without waiting for an answer: *Did I think justice had been done? When did I realize I'd lost a case I should have won?* The press would make the verdict about me when it wasn't. Sheila would live the rest of her life as a woman who falsely accused a well-respected man of rape to cover up her adulterous behavior. Regardless of what she said, *Daniel* would be the victim of her life story. The community would excuse him for having sex with a beautiful young woman on the floor of the classroom in which he taught teens history. But the same people would remember Sheila as the fallen woman, the temptress. If only we could make her wear a scarlet letter around her neck, justice would be served.

All speculation was about to end. Judge Tawney resumed his position on the bench. The jury filed in, and the formalities began. The judge asked the jury forewoman if they'd reached a verdict. The worst we should have expected was, "No." Some jurors might have doubts, but certainly not all.

Surprisingly, the jury forewoman answered the question in the affirmative. She was then asked to confirm the verdict was unanimous. It was.

The forewoman handed the verdict form to the clerk, who handed it to the judge, who handed it back to the clerk in what amounted to a form of legal ping-pong. And then the clerk's voice filled the courtroom. "As to the charge of sexual assault and battery, how does the jury find?"

The forewoman, a shapeless woman of indeterminate age, stood, her hand visibly shaking as she read from a slip of paper. "The jury finds Daniel Lockhart not guilty."

I heard Sheila inhale, then make a soft whimpering sound. She glanced and smiled at Helena, who was sitting a few rows behind us. Helena was steel-faced. She barely acknowledged her daughter and didn't show surprise or disappointment.

Sheila stood, whispered a thank you, then departed. Those remaining in attendance filed out slowly, leaving me alone in the vacuous chamber with my thoughts and second thoughts.

Even as I looked for excuses, a voice in my head was screaming the truth. *You lost the case because the jury didn't want to believe Sheila Fanning had been raped, particularly by Daniel Lockhart, a man who may have taught their children or helped build a playground in their neighborhood.* That was the reality. Without a confession or a witness to the attack, the circumstantial evidence would have had to be overwhelming to sway a jury of his peers to convict him. The slightest doubt and he would go free.

But that explanation wasn't satisfying. I was searching for another when I looked up from the prosecution table and saw Liz Chase glaring at me, her face distorted by deep furrows and a clenching jaw. For a moment, her rage denied her the ability to speak. But after a quick and noisy breath, she found her voice and vented her disappointment.

"It's one thing to be born female and to have to contend with all the inequities that come with our gender. But this…I've been advocating for women's rights for two decades…What the hell just happened?"

Liz was in her late fifties and had worked for presidents, universities, and a variety of women's organizations. She was an icon, a force to be reckoned with, and my friend. But to the extent her anger was directed at me, it was misdirected. She had pleaded with Sheila to file a complaint against Daniel—if not for her, for women everywhere. Liz's assertiveness surprised me, especially considering she must have known the trauma a rape trial could cause the victim. I had refrained from my usual bluntness, and in the end, the state attorney took the case to the grand jury.

I heard Liz sigh, after which she answered her own question.

"The jury had an excuse to doubt the sexual encounter was rape, and they let him go."

"That's the gist of it."

Liz gave me a sympathetic look. "Don't let the case eat at you," she said.

I said I wouldn't, a lie we both accepted at face value, and she exited the room. When I reached the courtroom door, Liz reappeared.

"I think I'm talked out," I said without making eye contact. "Right now, I have a date with a salty margarita, which I plan on drinking while soaking in water laced with lavender. Whatever it is, it can wait."

Liz grabbed my arm. "No, it can't wait! They've arrested her!"

"Who? What…arrested who?"

Liz gestured wildly with her hands. "Sheila! The state police were waiting for her when she left the courtroom. She's being held in a cell awaiting arraignment."

"Waiting for her? What? On what charge?"

"They're accusing her of violating the state law prohibiting abortion."

"I'm confused. How…"

My question answered itself. The rape resulted in a pregnancy Sheila chose to end. The state law prohibited abortion except in cases of rape, incest, and endangerment of the life of the mother.

"Are you okay?"

I nodded even as I tried to stop my heart from pounding in my ears. "I should have known she was pregnant after the rape," I said.

A silence ensued, a knowing moment in which a profound, if not obvious, realization gripped me.

"Someone had to know. Someone in the attorney general's office knew about her abortion before the trial. Why would she share that information with his office and not tell me?"

The answer was—she wouldn't.

Liz didn't seem to appreciate the implications of the observation, and I chose not to enlighten her. But as long as Sheila Fanning could claim she was raped, her abortion was legal under the state abortion law's exception for rape. With the verdict, she had lost that protection. Her immediate arrest meant the attorney general expected Daniel's acquittal and was prepared to argue that because Sheila's pregnancy was the product of consensual sex, her abortion was illegal.

In the blink of an eye, Sheila went from being a victim to becoming a defendant, transitioning from a woman who had been sexually assaulted to a woman who could face imprisonment for up to five years if convicted.

The timing of the not-guilty verdict and Sheila's arrest weren't a stunning piece of blind luck. Someone must have planned it. But by whom? How…? The questions made my head spin.

"What are you going to do about it?" asked Liz. I couldn't think about it, much less get involved in a postmortem with Liz. "Not now," I said and headed to the door, only to be stopped again, this time by the appearance of Phillip Dunlevy.

"I thought you did the best you could with the case you were given. Daniel was never going to be convicted. Not enough injury or violence, a stellar community reputation…all it took was giving the jury an excuse to acquit him. Don't beat yourself up because others will do that for you."

Liz wasn't in the mood to be gracious in defeat. "So, the basis of your defense was that rape turned her on physically, therefore she must have given her consent? You're a pig."

"Not how the jury saw it," countered Phillip. "Social media is touting Daniel as a victim of a woke campaign and a hero for sticking up for men who are at the mercy of lying women and woke female prosecutors. Not my take, but it's out there."

He looked at me, waiting for me to respond. When I didn't, he added, "I just came by to advise you I'll be filing a motion to have Daniel's DNA expunged from all state and federal databases. I hope you won't contest it."

Liz and I watched him leave, then saw Carl Hinton, the state attorney general, coming toward us.

"And the bad news keeps coming," said Liz.

"I need a word with Ashley," he said, then added, "alone."

Liz rolled her eyes and departed. Carl stood a few inches from my face, his breath wafting over me. I thought about stepping back but inched closer to him instead.

"I know how it is to lose a case," he said, "but you need to understand you're now in the public eye. In a few minutes, the governor and lieutenant governor will arrive. We will make statements for the press and you will join us. It would be inappropriate under the circumstances for you to show any remorse about the way the case was decided or displeasure about Sheila Fanning's arrest. Being a team player is a good career move. Are we clear?"

Not really. What did he mean, team player? Why would I express remorse or displeasure if the verdict was fair? What did my demeanor have to do with my career? And what did Phillip Dunlevy mean when he said Daniel would never be convicted?

Losing a case is one thing. I can deal with that, and maybe learn something in the process. But this case felt different. Even Sheila's mother felt it.

The alignment of the events—Daniel's acquittal and Sheila's arrest—seemed too perfect. Questioning the circumstances as anything other than fortuitous required believing the events weren't random, but planned and coordinated and then executed quietly, so no one would notice. The idea seemed far-fetched, but as I stared into the cold eyes of Carl Hinton, I could only wonder.

"Yes sir," I said. "Perfectly."

CHAPTER FIVE

To have the governor, lieutenant governor, and attorney general of the state in a small town at the same time was as unusual as it was telling. The reason was obvious: Sheila was about to become the star of a political drama produced for the antiabortion factions of the governor's base. I was window dressing, a bit-player added in hopes my presence would lend credibility to the occasion. Given the warning I'd received from the attorney general, he didn't trust me, but felt he needed me.

The Village of Freeman's Gate was an odd venue for such an important bit of political theater. With a population of 12,000—give or take—it had no political importance, with few having even heard of it.

The name of the town evokes images of a stop on the underground railway, but its actual origins are more mundane. Freeman was a merchant who built a fort to protect his store. The store was accessible by a large gate that became the landmark by which traders identified the store's location. Over time, the fort attracted other businesses, and the village soon outgrew the inner perimeter. The gate was removed to make way for a street, but the name stuck.

Freeman located his store on the eastern shore of the Piney River. As the town grew, the residents of Freeman's Gate had aspirations that the settlement would become a commercial center for trade in the two most important commodities of the nineteenth century: cotton and tobacco. To be fair, the promoters of this vision had a reason for optimism. The Piney River was navigable to the coast and with unlimited land to the west and slaves to provide free labor, the production of these crops was massively profitable and seemingly unlimited. Everyone profited, or at least those who were free.

But as often happens, greed blinds the eye to what, in hindsight, is obvious. In a decade, the productivity of the land was in decline. Perhaps harder to recognize was that the clearing of the land along the river had increased the silt that flowed into it. All this became clear when two years of drought not only ruined the crops but made the river unusable for heavy barges. One by one, the tobacco and cotton warehouses closed. A few caught fire in what was largely recognized as a scheme to collect insurance money.

Before the crops failed and the drought rendered the river unnavigable, the city fathers built a magnificent courthouse of stone and marble. There was talk that the Village could be a candidate for the new state capital. The courthouse was a symbol of the future, a future that never came.

An expensive and stunning structure, the courthouse was also a reminder that building something no one asked for wasn't a strategy for urban development. With the failure of the cotton and tobacco businesses, the town languished. The money gravitated to the big urban cities, and the workers followed suit. State colleges drew students and research facilities to other regions. What could the Village offer?

The answer, which took decades to be appreciated, was a quality of life and, ironically, a courthouse that no one was using. Working in big cities is one thing, but living in them and raising a family is another. In the late eighties, communities sprung up outside the old town center that attracted young professionals who didn't mind commuting to the cities for work. Then, money flowed into the small town and the Village sprouted quaint shops, restaurants, and bistros that attracted tourists and suburbanites alike. Freeman's Gate was reborn as a smaller version of Williamsburg or Savannah, a place where all were welcome. Until recently, the reality lived up to the marketing pitch.

The town's location made this renaissance possible. To the east was the state capital. To the west was the state university. In between the Village and these institutions, a variety of high-tech parks and research facilities were constructed. Locals primarily used the newly constructed parkways, making the Village easily accessible for commuters. From an infrastructure perspective, the Village was a perfect place to live.

When a fire destroyed the courthouse at the county seat, the attorney general's office moved the state attorney's office from the fifth district to Freeman's Gate. The move was supposed to be temporary, but as appropriations for funds to replace the burned-out structure languished in the legislature, more and more of the prosecutors and staff took up permanent residence in the Village. Twenty years later, no one was moving.

Sadly, the last few years have brought political and social discord to this once quiet and friendly place. The city council meetings became a venue for voicing grievances and conspiracy theories at the expense of facts and loving thy neighbor. Groups petitioned the school board and library to remove an assortment of books, claiming the history taught to me is now too offensive and "woke" to be taught to Harper. The arrest of Sheila Fanning was just one more stain on the town's loving reputation.

The attorney general directed me to stand behind Governor Warren Adams and the Lieutenant Governor, Tanya Hobbs, who stood at a podium flanked by a half-dozen state troopers. The group watched as the media assembled in front of them. Given that a rape trial in the hinterlands wasn't exactly national news, I surmised that the governor's office had summoned the press after the verdict of not guilty was official, and that reporters were only now arriving from other venues.

The governor's office had chosen the location of the podium, so the front of the courthouse would appear in all the photographs and videos of the press conference. The magnificent building sits high on a half-mile-wide plaza reached by three flights of stairs. It exudes power and even arrogance. By implication, a man standing here had to be important.

Behind the press, a few dozen onlookers were milling about. They carried signs and posters, but not in a way that I could discern what they were advocating.

Governor Adams started the event by welcoming everyone to the Village, clasping both hands together, lifting them face high, giving them a shake, and announcing, "This is a special day."

The words brought the small crowd to life. Signs and posters were raised and prominently displayed so the media could see and photograph them. The basic theme was to promote the protection of the unborn by outlawing abortion.

Curiously, one sign read:

"RAPE ISN'T THE FAULT OF THE UNBORN."

Another read:

"DON'T PUNISH THE UNBORN FOR THE SINS OF THE MOTHER."

Taken together, the message seemed to be that the assault was Sheila's fault and, by allowing the assault, she had somehow sinned.

Governor Adams quieted his supporters, then continued.

"As you know, my administration has advocated to make this state safer for women, regardless of economic status or political affiliation. Before I introduce Attorney General Hinton, I'd like to announce that as part of this initiative, we have completed the testing phase of our rape kit backlog clearance project. Over ten thousand of these kits have been languishing in evidence warehouses throughout the state. I have appointed Ashley Corbin…" he turned and nodded toward me… "to manage the last phase of this project. Shortly, we will begin uploading the DNA data from the testing phase to our databases so we can begin matching these signatures to known perpetrators."

He again turned and smiled at me as a smattering of applause rippled through the plaza, albeit more polite than enthusiastic. The appointment surprised me, but I nodded and smiled back in my new role as a dutiful toady.

"But…but that's not all that makes this day special. While I have taken the initiative to protect the rights of women, I have also promised to protect the rights of the unborn. Most recently, my administration, through the dedicated advocacy of our Lieutenant Governor, Tanya Cobb, has reaffirmed its commitment to enforcing the abortion law that protected the unborn for decades before the decision in *Roe*. With the decision reversed, I promised to enforce vigorously the abortion provisions of the state criminal code once again. Today…"

The demonstrators erupted with a chant of "no more abortions," their voices blending and echoing into the air, punctuated by loud cheers.

"…today we have made it clear that the exceptions for rape and incest will not be used to bypass the clear intent of the law that abortion is a felony, and that we will punish violators—those who perform abortions and those who procure them—accordingly. Attorney General Hinton will explain what we have done today in greater detail, but I think it should be clear that this state, under my administration, will not let the murder of babies go unpunished any longer."

The lieutenant governor joined the governor and together, they basked in cheers from the dancing, poster-waving crowd.

I had met Tanya once. Curiously, the attorney general invited her to a meeting to discuss whether to charge Daniel Lockhart. I found her arrogance and condescending attitude off-putting. Worse, she struck me as one of those women who was told as a child how pretty she was and now, thirty years and fifty pounds later, still believed it. I accepted that the thought was petty, but enjoyed it anyway.

The attorney general had instructed me to maintain a professional demeanor. In particular, I was to hide my emotional reaction to the not-guilty verdict in the case of Daniel Lockhart and Sheila Fanning's arrest. While the instruction was annoyingly arrogant, I was more than happy to comply. I was eager to escape the media circus and avoid being questioned about my thoughts and feelings out of concern for what I might say if cornered.

While the politicians continued basking in their victory over sin and evil, I took stock of the facts as I saw them. In a strict legal sense, Daniel Lockhart had received justice. The state, meaning me, hadn't proved beyond a reasonable doubt that his actions justified taking away his liberty. But to use that failure of proof as a basis for concluding he hadn't raped Sheila was a legal non sequitur. The jury may have had doubts about whether she consented to sex, but they didn't affirmatively find that she did. Factually, Daniel could have raped Sheila, but the evidence simply wasn't sufficient to meet the legal standard for conviction.

To be fair, the doctor who performed the abortion couldn't independently determine whether she'd been raped. The attending healthcare providers had to rely solely on Sheila's assertion she'd been sexually assaulted, which was supported by the nurse's examination and the police report of the incident at the school.

No matter what the law says or means, it is to be applied rationally. Charging Sheila with a felony seemed unnecessarily cruel. That Tanya and her associates didn't care was telling.

The attorney general announced Sheila's arrest under the abortion law of 1932 to a cheering crowd. I did my best to look emotionally detached, only to find myself imagining I was watching a modern-day witch trial. All that was missing were pitchforks, people in funny hats and shoes, and flaming torches. The mental pictures of a crowd yelling, "Kill the witch," invited a smile to my lips, a response I quickly quelled.

When the attorney general thanked the crowd, I thought the spectacle was over. But as he backed away from the microphones, two state troopers appeared from the courthouse. Between them was Sheila, handcuffs on her wrists, her face portraying bewilderment at her current circumstance. As Sheila was perp-walked toward the press corps, I saw Tanya Cobb beaming with joy, unable to feel any empathy for this unfortunate woman.

I had always seen the courthouse, with its stately facade, as a testament to justice, law, and fairness. But today, I realized it was an illusion, like a soldier who wears a uniform adorned with medals for battles he never fought. Nothing that happened today was about justice, humanity, or compassion.

As I watched Sheila being pushed into a waiting police car, I imagined myself stepping forward and demanding that they set her free or even lying in front of the police car in defiance of the governor. But as the police car drove away, an empty feeling overcame me, and I realized that helping Sheila was beyond my reach. She had become a prisoner of a political machine that had no intention of letting her go.

CHAPTER SIX

With the spectacle over, I quickly left the plaza, relieved to have avoided publicly venting my rage about the trial and Sheila's arrest.

I was of two minds. The most comforting was to go home, tend to my bruised self-esteem with a cocktail or a glass of wine, and think about something else. It was a good plan. The other was to find Helena and see whether I could explain what had happened in a way that didn't make me feel like a complete failure. This option was the least desirable but the most appropriate under the circumstances.

A text from the State Attorney, Martin Hudson, summoning me to an urgent meeting spared me from having to choose.

Voters had elected Martin on a platform for enforcing the law fairly but compassionately. He wouldn't coddle criminals but if someone made a mistake and could be spared from the criminal system, he was open to considering any mitigating circumstances. I liked Martin and his approach, especially for young, first-time offenders. Others found this approach weak, so much so that they attacked him on social media as "the woke prosecutor," whatever that meant. Over the last year, his decisions not to prosecute certain cases put him at odds with the attorney general's office. The political pressure made him cautious, an attitude I encountered when I'd advocated against charging Daniel Lockhart.

The state attorney's office was on the fourth floor of the courthouse. I left the elevator in a don't-speak-to-me frame of mind. The normally chatty receptionist read my mood and buzzed me into the office suite without saying a word. The moment the door opened, the hum of voices stopped, and my office mates turned their heads to look at me. Their expressions conveyed support and compassion.

An observer might have thought I'd just received news of a death in the family. The observer might have had the circumstances wrong, but not the emotion. Losing a high-profile case was a shared experience. Many of my office mates had helped with legal research and fact-gathering. Several had volunteered to take part in a mini-trial to test ways of shaping testimony. The gloom of defeat was as much theirs as mine.

I continued to my office and shut the door. For a moment, I sat at my desk and shuffled the messages that were stacked on my keyboard. The most important message reminded me of a video conference call at four to discuss the status of the rape kit backlog elimination project. I did a quick computer search and learned that over the last few decades, tens of thousands of samples taken from rape victims had remained untested. The legislature had finally funded a massive project to test these samples, generically referred to as "rape kits," to eliminate the backlog and hopefully find and arrest perpetrators. It was unclear what they expected me to contribute to this process, but I recorded the meeting time and login information on my phone.

I ignored the list of new emails and surfed to a live broadcast from CNN. Since I'd left the courthouse plaza, a satellite truck had arrived and was providing coverage of a group of protestors that had assembled to exchange taunts with the pro-governor crowd. The newcomers weren't as prepared or organized as their opponents, but the language they used was much more colorful.

The CNN commentator described the scene in a tense voice that conveyed a sense of impending violence, something that would certainly be good for ratings and late-night news junkies. But for the moment, the word exchanges seemed more like two cats yowling at each other from a distance than a soon-to-be-fought riot over differing values.

Back in the studio, the anchor asked Brooke Hastings, a former prosecutor, her thoughts about the trial of Sheila Fanning:

"I'm always reluctant to second-guess lawyers after a trial, but of course, that's what you're asking me to do.

"First, I have no doubt this particular woman was selected to test the rape exception to the state's abortion law. We don't know how this was orchestrated but we know that the governor and lieutenant governor were quickly ushered to Freeman's Gate following the verdict. We also know that the rape trial was assigned to an inexperienced attorney. That said, I thought the prosecutor did a good job.

"Rape cases make juries uncomfortable because testimony and evidence involve talking about intimate acts, intimate parts of the body, and physiology that few people understand in depth. I thought the prosecutor made the case for rape, but the jury just seemed to tune out the evidence against consent, focusing on the fact that the rape victim was aroused even as she feared for her life as evidence of consent. Women are still being punished for their anatomy.

"Of course, Governor Adams' national reputation will be improved by the perception that the rape trial was unwarranted and how he turned the tables on an accuser who was using rape as a shield for her illegal abortion. That said, I think it's a sad day for women's rights and justice generally. Doctors are already reluctant to provide care to women experiencing miscarriages or prenatal complications. This prosecution will end any medical treatment for pregnant women that risks the life of the fetus."

I heard a quick knock on my door just before it flew open and Martin Hudson stepped in.

"Brooke Hastings said some nice things about me," I said without looking up. "She said I was inexperienced, which I'm not, but made up for her error by saying I did a good job. Curiously, she said the arrest of Sheila Fanning looked,"—I made air quotes— "orchestrated. Interesting choice of words, don't you think?"

He closed the door and approached my desk. "It is…"

"It suggests someone has been changing the rules of the game. Personally, I think you haven't been honest with me."

"Honest? What…"

"You know, for one, it might have been helpful for me to know Sheila Fanning had an abortion. The AG obviously knew. I don't want to believe you knew and didn't share, but at the moment, I'm not feeling like I can trust anyone."

Martin pulled a chair up to my desk and sat down. He wove his fingers together in a prayer position, made a steeple with his index fingers, and touched them to his lips. I never liked this affectation, but for no reason I could express. Perhaps he thought it made him look erudite, but mostly, I found it tedious.

"Okay. I sense you're angry, but I need you to cut the attitude."

"Attitude? Is that what you sense? How about betrayal? How about trusting your superiors to give you the tools to do your job? How about—"

"Stop! For Christ's sake. Shut up and listen to me."

Martin momentarily buried his face in his hands, took a breath, and exhaled slowly. "Just listen. We've both been played—me maybe more than you. I told you what I knew about the case. I wasn't advised Sheila had gotten pregnant or had an abortion. Only as the case was proceeding to trial did I overhear Governor Adams and Attorney General Hinton talking about it."

I stared at him silently and watched him squirm.

"Honestly. I thought you knew. I mean, if Sheila told them, I assumed she told you. But no one told me or I would have made that fact known to you. So, no, I didn't betray you. I wouldn't do that. But what you have to get into your head is that this office has to operate in the reality that surrounds us. I didn't create it. Time will tell if this is what the voters wanted, but that's not something we can control. Maybe all this bullshit will fade away, but for now, we have to deal with it."

"How is dealing with it going to help Sheila?"

Martin answered with a shrug. "She is a victim in a social war that threatens to bury people like you and me. What happens to her doesn't matter…"

"Doesn't matter?" I leaned forward and tapped my desk with my finger. "We barely know who Sheila is, what her dreams were, how she imagined her life. We will only remember her as the woman who alleged she'd been raped, and the first woman to be charged this century under an ancient abortion law. She lost everything, and her assailant walked away free. That may not matter to you, but it does to me."

"Of course it matters to me. What I'm telling you is we can't change any of that. We need to accept the facts as they are and fight the next battle."

I stared at him and scoffed. "You can't imagine what it's like to be raped or to have to decide whether to abort a child!"

"And you can?"

The question was probably rhetorical, a casual retort delivered in the course of an argument for which an answer wasn't expected. But its impact on me was anything but casual. I glared at Martin so hard he flinched, only to realize I hadn't offered him a denial.

"Sorry. That was inappropriate on all levels. I'm making a mess of this and I'm sorry. I'm trying to explain we're on the same page and it's not coming out right. Please forgive me."

The look on Martin's face made me feel sorry for him. He had unintentionally asked the right question and learned more than he wanted to know or that I wanted to tell him. My secret, like all secrets, wanted to escape the prison I'd locked it in. I had kept it contained for fifteen years. The trial and the arrest of Sheila Fanning had opened an old wound. Daniel Lockhart's victory smile, the joyful face of Lieutenant Governor Tanya Cobb, and the glee with which she welcomed the persecution of Sheila Fanning had taken a toll on my vigilance. My non-response was telling and no amount of explanation was going to untell it.

We fell into an awkward silence, hovering outside the boundaries of our old relationship and struggling to define what it would be going forward. Martin looked at his hands, something he did when he was thinking. Thankfully, he didn't ask for an explanation, and I didn't volunteer one.

After a few minutes, he lifted his head. "When speaking in public, I say the right things about the law being fair and justice blind, but is it just empty sound bites? The moral high ground can be a lonely place because the people who can get you what you want aren't living there. What do people in public service do when they're asked to choose between their values and their future, between what is right and the things they want? That choice is coming to this office if it hasn't already arrived."

"Martin…"

"Let me finish. The idea of an unwed, successful mother leading their campaign against abortion fascinates the governor, and especially the lieutenant governor. The attorney general and Tanya Cobb just asked me to assign Sheila's abortion case to you. They see you as a single woman who chose to have a child. They seem to think you would be okay with prosecuting her on the abortion charge. You would become the face of the new politics of this state. You couldn't write a script for a story like that because no one would believe it. Imagine you're in court prosecuting a young woman for killing her baby. The spectacle would draw national attention, raising the governor's stature with his base and our stature with him. All you have to do is ditch your moral principles and join the winning side."

He read the anger on my face, but before I could verbalize my displeasure, he rolled his eyes and laughed. "I'm insensitive sometimes, but even I have my limits." When I didn't respond, he said, "This would be the place where you would say I'm not insensitive and maybe add a few words to soothe my ego."

I crossed my arms over my chest and leaned back in my chair. "Apparently, I'm not in an ego-soothing mood. More to the point, what happens when I say no?"

Martin reverted to his praying pose. "You don't have to. I refused because it would be a conflict for you to defend her in one case and prosecute her in another. At least, that was the excuse I offered."

"Spit it out, Martin. What aren't you telling me?"

"The governor wants everyone to sign a loyalty oath, swearing we will collectively and individually support the governor's policies and represent those policies in court when asked. They are actively looking into the backgrounds of civil servants to identify potential enemies. They have already approached me about something in my past that might interest the bar association. I'm sure they're looking at you. Saying anything that expresses displeasure over the decision to prosecute Sheila will only heighten their suspicion about your loyalty to their cause."

"Can they do that?"

"Not legally. But when you control the institutions that would normally stop you, you can get away with pretty much anything."

The silence returned, accompanied by a heavy gloom and thoughts about how quickly life changes.

I snickered softly, and Martin gave me a puzzled look.

"This situation feels like a movie scene where two soldiers huddle in a burned-out basement, their ammunition depleted, strategizing about how to survive against an approaching army of mutant roaches. I guess this is what hopelessness feels like."

"Mutant roaches?" He laughed. "Seems apt."

"Understand, no matter what these hateful people do, I won't sign anything, and I won't prosecute Sheila for a crime only a woman can commit. Tell the governor and his puppets to go to hell."

Martin shrugged. "That would be at least momentarily satisfying, but sadly not likely to accomplish much. I'm not sure if we have options, but if we do, that isn't one of them. What I was trying to say before I stepped on my tongue was we need to appear unaffected by Sheila's prosecution. I'll take the abortion case myself and try to buy us some time."

"To do what?"

"See if you can find any legal maneuver that will help Sheila Fanning, even if we have to break a few rules. And most importantly, don't trust anyone in this office. We can text via Blind Eye. It's encrypted. I'll send you an invitation. It may sound silly but get a burner phone. Don't buy it with your credit card. The best place is a gas station convenience store being watched by a kid, preferably with pimples. Turn off your regular phone before you get anywhere near the place you buy the burner and ideally find a store that doesn't have a security camera near the counter."

"Jesus, Martin. That's like cool and scary at the same time."

Martin laughed. "Maybe I hang out with criminals too much."

"Burner phone and encryption app. Got it. Next on my list: Phillip Dunlevy said he was going to move to expunge Daniel Lockhart's DNA data from the state databases. Your thoughts?"

"I'm guessing it's just a procedural thing his lawyer came up with. He's a libertarian and thinks the government knows too much about us. I'm sympathetic to the argument, but you should look into it to see if there's something more to it. I'll trust your judgment on how we should respond. Anything else?"

Martin was at the door before I could answer. "Did you find the timing of the verdict and Sheila's arrest a bit…convenient?"

"Please don't go there."

"I don't want to, but as Brooke Hastings said, it seems…orchestrated. Planned even."

Martin leaned against the doorjamb. "Okay, I'll agree it's tempting. But consider what it would take to orchestrate something like this. To ensure an acquittal, you would need the judge and the jury to be involved and you would need to keep it a secret. That's just TV fiction."

"What if you weren't looking for a particular outcome but just wanted to improve the odds?"

"That's a lot of trouble to go to just to gain an advantage." He took a step toward me. "I know what happens when a thought gets rattling around in that head of yours. Tell me you'll let this one die silently. Pursuing it will just bring us more grief."

I nodded in apparent agreement, and the door closed. I stared blankly at my computer monitor, at the images of talking heads on CNN. The sound was muted, but the closed captions scrolled across the bottom of the screen. Mostly, I was seeing but not paying attention.

The scene suddenly changed to a live video of the street that fronted the courthouse plaza. Sign-carrying groups, some who favored arresting Sheila Fanning and some opposed, confronted state police dressed in riot gear. A text from Tanya Cobb imploring "the soldiers of God" to "strike down sinners and the disciples of the devil" had stoked the tensions. The police struggled to keep the factions separated, although it appeared from the pictures they were more willing to club the pro-Sheila protestors than those celebrating her arrest.

The new American reality had made its way to the Village.

Lisa Calloway, the front desk receptionist, appeared at my door. "You've got a visitor. I think she's Sheila Fanning's mother. I can tell her you're busy."

As I refocused on what mattered, a feeling of dread overwhelmed me. Explaining to Helena how Daniel Lockhart was acquitted was difficult. Explaining Sheila's arrest seemed impossible.

I sighed audibly. "No. I'll come out."

Helena Davis stood and greeted me with a smile, something that surprised me. As I approached, I felt her eyes on me, her welcoming gaze masking whatever thoughts or feelings she might have been wrestling with.

"Getting arrested wasn't one of the options we discussed," she said. "If you have time, I'd like to get your thoughts on what happens now."

"I'm sorry…"

"Don't go there. Nothing that happened was your fault. What we need to do now is identify Sheila's options and see where that takes us."

I grabbed my briefcase and phone. "I can't think in here. Let's go for a walk."

I led Helena to Freedom Park, a small enclave of trees and ponds on the west side of the Village I frequented when needing to escape my thoughts and the opinions of others.

En route, we took turns sharing the simple facts that revealed who we were. Helena's life was far more interesting than mine. She was an alpaca rancher and a famous one at that. She ran the business by herself, her husband having died when Sheila was only ten. I offered a polite "I'm sorry" that prompted a shocking clarification.

"I lived in Tuberville with my husband, Darnel. He was a Black man, which wasn't common in those parts. When police went looking for an escaped prisoner, the first non-white man they found was Darnel. He was working in an old barn and looked like he was hiding out. They claimed he refused to comply with their instructions, but there were no witnesses to say one way or the other and shot him dead. Later, they found the escaped prisoner passed out in a laundry truck next to a jar of prison moonshine. The Tuberville police department's lawyer gave me the choice of taking a pile of money or fighting them in court for years. Against everything I believed, I took the money and moved to Sumner. Sheila and I have managed on our own since until this business in Freeman's Gate."

"The police killed him? Jesus."

A moment passed, after which I stopped and faced her.

"Did you say alpacas?"

"Darnel was a clever man. Tobacco and cotton had ruined the soil for farming. Cattle ranching was too expensive. The market for sheep's wool was volatile, like wheat. The new thing was alpaca wool. It's expensive to process but more sustainable. So, he purchased some land in Sumner and fixed up an old barn. His first alpacas were a breeding pair. He started networking with other alpaca ranchers. He saw the long term and was patient. After his death, I moved to Sumner with Sheila and learned everything I could about alpacas. I invested the payoff money in equipment and stock. Thankfully, my flock produced highly rated wool, and soon, I had repeat orders. Maybe his death made his dream possible. Life is like that. I still miss him and now I miss Sheila. Hard to know why my life is what it is, but you play the hand you're dealt."

The park was empty. To my relief, Helena was patient, saving her questions for the right moment. If I had been in her shoes, I'm not sure I'd have the same willpower. We found a bench on the north side of the lake and watched waterfowl navigate the water's edge in search of food. The sun warmed my face, and for a merciful ten minutes, I gave into the sheer pleasure of observing life free of human agendas and the demands they spawned. But musing over the quacks, honks, and chatters of ducks and geese could only delay the inevitable for so long.

"Did you sit through the whole trial?" I asked.

"I did. This morning, I left home early, hoping to speak with Sheila before the trial started, but I arrived just as the judge sat down. Liz had saved me a seat."

"I wish I…"

"Sheila said you were against going to trial. I was the one who insisted she fight back. I didn't have to because she's stubborn like me. So, you have nothing to apologize for."

"Did you know about her abortion?"

"I paid for it. No way she's bringing the child of a rapist into this world. She didn't tell you because she didn't want her husband, Quinn, to find out. But that's water over the dam. I want to understand what her options are. I don't have the money to spend on lawyers. She's living hand to mouth because Quinn is unemployed and won't take a job he thinks is beneath him. He's pigheaded that way. Can she fight the charges and win?"

"To be clear, my office will prosecute her. It would be inappropriate…"

A noisy kerfuffle involving two male ducks who were vying for the attention of a female stopped me. The female duck wanted nothing to do with either of the male ducks, but that didn't stop them from making lots of noise and fighting over her.

"You were saying?"

I laughed. "I was going to throw out a lot of legal babble and say nothing. Here's how I see it. The overruling of *Roe* revived the old abortion law. Lots of these morality laws remain on the books but are never enforced. For fifty years, the state's abortion law was a zombie, not dead but not alive either. The law prohibits abortions except in cases of rape, incest and for protecting the life of the mother. The state has already used the courts to intimidate doctors from relying on the life of the mother exception. I think the governor and his political machine are prosecuting Sheila and her doctor to make abortions based on a claim of rape too risky for both patient and doctor. Basically, they are intent on reading the exceptions out of the statute even though the legislature refused to amend the law."

"What does that mean for Sheila?"

"My guess is that the attorney general will torment Sheila for a while and then allow her to plead guilty to a felony. Whether sending her to prison is in the cards depends on how they read public opinion. If she wants to fight the charges, they will certainly tell her that once she pleads not guilty, all offers are off the table. She will either have to win or they will lock her up for five years."

"Can she win?"

"She should have won today. I don't know. Maybe, but it depends on whether the state plays fair." I glanced at Helena, then shook my head. "No. She can't win because the state has no intention of playing fair. I don't have any proof, but I think the state has had its thumb on the scale of justice this whole time. I wish I knew how, but I think charging Sheila under the abortion law was the why."

Helena patted my hand. "Now I know why Sheila admires you so much. You've got a good heart and you speak your mind." She stood and handed me a card. "I'm going to see if I can visit her before I leave, but you can call or text me on this number. Thank you for your time."

•   •   •

Helena was still in view when I realized I had stepped over a line, even if just a little. It wasn't my place to speculate on how the state would prosecute Sheila on the abortion charge. I tried to imagine how she would decide whether to take a plea for a crime she didn't commit or to fight the charges and face spending the next five years of her life in state prison. The exercise did nothing but make me angry.

My options weren't so binary. Martin was adamant that we needed to avoid confronting powerful men and women, people who often said one thing and believed another. But questions haunted me, questions with no obvious answers: How could the governor and his minions have been so confident Daniel would be acquitted? Why wasn't Daniel more aggressive about delaying or even postponing his trial? What was going on with the jury? Was Quinn's departure from the courthouse planned?

I was no match for the governor, the lieutenant governor, or the attorney general. Courage is a great attribute, but what's the point in picking a fight you can't win? How do you live with yourself if you don't?

Martin had framed the choice as choosing between my values and my future, between what is right and what I wanted. What I wanted most was for someone else to save her, for a clever defense attorney or a fair-minded judge to set her free. But what if there was no one else?

CHAPTER SEVEN

Melancholy filled my walk home, a sadness that felt like mourning, but without the requisite dead person. I saw the town I called home differently. Perhaps detached would best describe it? The Village was the place where I came to heal, the place where I raised my daughter. But now, the polarizing dogma that had gripped the country had cast its shadow here, spreading and thriving. The advocates of this dogma rejected the notion of the collective good in favor of a singular belief system, one that had to be imposed at any cost. Even the state attorney was afraid of them.

My house is on a quiet, tree-lined street a few blocks from the downtown corridor. I'm not sure if there is a name for the architectural style of the houses in my neighborhood. Some say people purchased most of the houses from catalogs published by Sears and Roebuck in the nineteen twenties. Whatever its origins—with its covered front porch, green shutters, and perfectly shaped magnolia tree in the front yard—it exudes coziness. Just the sight of it pulled me from my gloom.

It was just after two. For a half-hour, I would have the house to myself. My daughter, Harper, would arrive before three and, undoubtedly well-versed in the morning's events and social media commentary about the trial and me, ready to share her opinions about all of it regardless of whether I wanted to hear them.

I took advantage of the solitude to scan dozens of voicemails, emails, and texts from media outlets seeking comments on the trial verdict and Sheila Fanning's subsequent arrest. Instead of answering them, I elected to reheat a large portion of leftover lasagna and pour a glass of wine.

I was preparing for my four o'clock conference call when the front door swung open and was characteristically slammed shut.

Harper popped into the kitchen and glared at me. "What are you doing at home? Are you okay?"

She stood above me, her five-foot-seven frame caressed by a tight sweater and jeans. I was struck by how mature she looked, as if I'd missed her transition from child to beautiful young woman.

"Everything's fine, sweetie," I said softly, hoping to allay her anxiety. "There's another pan of lasagna in the refrigerator. I finished the wine, but happily, there's another bottle in the cooler. Not something you needed to know, but I said it anyway."

"Are you like drunk or something?"

I shrugged and smiled. "I don't know. Maybe something is about right. I finished a bottle, which is a strong suggestion I might be tipsy. I'll try to pretend to be sober. As I'm sure you know, I've had a shitty day, and it's not over yet."

"Do you know what people are saying about you online?"

"I don't, and probably don't want to, but give me the gist of it, minus the bad words."

"They are saying you screwed up the trial on purpose because you're a friend of the governor and that you helped get Mr. Lockhart off because you're having sex with him."

I laughed, spewing a spray of wine across the table. "The idea that I was part of a conspiracy against Sheila is hard enough to contemplate, but sex with Daniel Lockhart—I'm sure I would have remembered that, and not in a good way."

My mirthful moment passed quickly, replaced by a surge of anger. "What do these morons know?" I said, my voice quaking. I took in a deep breath and rubbed my eyes.

"Mom, I'm sorry…"

I emitted a long, loud groan, followed by a half-hearted laugh. "No need. I'm the one who should apologize. Please forgive me. It's the wine…There's nothing funny about what happened today. I trying to cope by being sarcastic. I'm just not good at it."

Harper sat down. "Tell me what happened."

I cradled my wineglass in both hands while I gathered my thoughts.

"It's fashionable to believe that some group or other is plotting against you when things don't go your way, but I can't shake the feeling there was a conspiracy of sorts. The judge, facts that Sheila neglected to tell me…I don't know. I lost and I shouldn't have. Maybe I'm not as good a lawyer as I like to think. I met her mother, Helena. I want to help Sheila, but it's not my job. She's not my client. Even if I wanted to, I have little to work with. I'm caught between my conscience and my professional responsibility. Even if tried to help her, I'd probably lose."

I closed my eyes and shook my head. "God, I sound so pathetic. Sheila deserves better than that. You have my permission to ignore your mother, which you do most of the time, anyway," I said. "That was funny in a sad way, don't you think?"

"Why do they want to put her in jail?"

"Because… I don't know. She had an abortion in violation of state law. That's now a crime. The governor wants to make an example of her, so women who are raped won't seek abortions and doctors won't perform them. It's unbelievable, isn't it?"

"So the governor would have forced Sheila to have the baby of the man who attacked her?"

The question, raw in its innocence, unleashed a flood of memories and old feelings loosened by wine and exhaustion. It was, oddly, ironic that I was looking at a child whose life, if I'd listened to my parents, would have ended before it began. I steeled myself against the rantings of my ghosts, determined not to make the mistake with Harper I'd made with Martin.

"It sure looks that way. I'm not sure if the driving force is Tanya Cobb, the Lieutenant Governor, or the governor himself. Anyway, the abortion law has exceptions for rape, protecting the life of the mother, and incest, which the pro-life folks don't like. The pro-choice crowd doesn't understand how ineffectual the exceptions are. But that doesn't matter in Sheila's case because the attorney general believes Daniel Lockhart's acquittal means she wasn't raped and, consequently, her abortion wasn't legal because she never qualified for the exception. I could argue to the contrary, but then you would leave, and I would be talking to myself."

"That's not right."

"I don't think it is, but my opinion doesn't count, you see, so it is a moot point. Some people say mute instead of moot, just so you know."

Harper folded her arms, ignored my attempt at humor, and gave me a serious look. "Is Sheila going to prison?"

"The case is in the hands of Carl Hinton, your Attorney General, who is friendly with Tanya Cobb, your Lieutenant Governor. If Tanya gets her way, Sheila will serve time. Actually, Tanya would probably like to see her executed, which, of course, is a tenet of a right-to-life philosophy."

"Being all snarky doesn't make you cool. Well, it's kind of cool when it's funny. That wasn't."

"Some kids were lucky to get cool parents. You, well, you got me. Luck of the draw."

"I might not have always thought so, but I think you're growing on me. I just don't want you to get down because of what happened. It wasn't your fault."

"I just had my ass kicked in court and had to watch a rapist walk free, then stand idle as the police arrested my victim. I'm home in the afternoon, feeling sorry for myself, possibly inebriated, and being consoled by my fifteen-year-old daughter. Not sure what to make of it." I reached over and patted her cheek. "Unless you have something more to say, I have work to do."

I again focused my attention on my computer while the microwave heated Harper's lasagna. When I was alone, I made coffee and logged into the conference call website. A pop-up on my screen advised that the meeting would begin when the moderator logged in and told me to be patient. While waiting, I reviewed material about the official history and objectives of the Rape Kit Backlog Elimination Task Force.

The governor's public relations machinery heralded the task force as "one of many initiatives to support women's rights." Despite what the "about" tab on the task force website stated, the truth was something else. The governor previously vetoed the law that created the task force because it was a waste of time and money to revisit old rape cases where the victims and perpetrators had moved on, the evidence had degraded, and the likelihood of convictions was low. Supporters of the governor were deriding the testing as a "woke" exercise, whatever that meant. When abortion became illegal again, the administration pointed to the task force as proof that it wasn't anti-women. The governor reversed his position, demanded a few minor changes to the statute, and then signed the measure at a press event surrounded by a large group of fawning supporters.

I made a few notes of what I might say on the conference call, not because I thought I would have something important to add to the discussion, but to make sure I said nothing I'd have to explain later.

My computer screen flickered and the faces of Francis Akins, an advisor in the governor's office, and Nora Barlow, the head of the State Forensic Lab for Genetic Testing, appeared. I knew and liked Nora, having worked with her on several cases. I had only seen Francis at a few social functions but viewed her with suspicion. She was often in the company of Tanya Cobb and Judge Tawney, which was, at least after today, enough to put her on my shit list.

Nora looked at her watch. "Let's get started. I need to explain a few things before we discuss the status of the rape kit project to be certain we are on the same page."

A slide depicting the various databases containing DNA samples filled the screen. Nora narrated to be certain we grasped the meaning of the various boxes.

"DNA is taken from crime scenes, from people who are arrested for crimes, and from victims of crimes. These crime scene data, what we call forensic data, and data from people arrested for crimes, what is sometimes referred to as criminal offender data, are in separate databases. The data from rape kits are crime scene data because victims of sexual assaults are, well, crime scenes. When a sexual assault case is opened, an officer may authorize a query of the criminal offender database to see if we can match the DNA left at the crime scene with a known person, someone who was previously arrested and tested. You know all this, but it's important to hear it again to understand the magnitude of the problem I'm facing. Questions?"

I shook my head. Francis, seemingly oblivious that Nora had stopped talking, continued to stare at her phone.

With a quick nod, Nora continued her monologue. "We have collected the useable DNA results from the old rape kits. Before uploading the data to the DNA database, we need to verify that it isn't corrupted and correctly formatted. We have also changed the database software to make it more compatible with other states and the FBI. We had a software glitch a few years ago that introduced errors into the matching system, so we are very careful before we go live."

"That sounds reasonable," I said. "So, when will the testing be done?"

"We have completed the testing protocol for the twenty-five hundred samples and reviewed the efficacy of the data to determine which data are usable. We should finish sorting the rape kit data to determine whether it shows multiple matches for single perpetrators—in other words, whether the data suggest the existence of serial rapists."

Francis, who appeared to have been focusing on something on her desk, snapped to attention.

"It is imperative that I approve any characterization of the rape kit data before it's released publicly. Is that clear?"

Nora said it was, and Francis left the call. I expected Nora to log off as well, but she continued to stare into the camera, her eyes betraying a simmering anger.

"Is there something you want to say to me?" I asked. "I mean, you look angry. Everyone seems angry with me today, so go for it."

Nora turned her gaze away from her camera. "It's not you. It's this job. Sometimes it just feels like what I do doesn't matter."

"You solve crimes. That's pretty awesome."

Suddenly, her face filled my screen. "It's bullshit. We didn't test ten thousand kits because time and storage conditions had degraded much of the evidence. Testing degraded samples is costly and requires extra processing. We discarded those kits and counted them as cleared. What we ended up with was data from a few thousand samples."

She buried her face in her hands, emitted a soft groan, then recovered. "I think we owe rape victims more. We have other tools to look for perpetrators, but we aren't allowed to use them. All this hoopla over eliminating the rape kit backlog is a political stunt, not serious law enforcement. Victims of sexual assault have suffered enough. At least we could be honest with them."

She took a long breath and let it out slowly. "Sorry about the rant. I'm just so tired of playing games with people's lives."

"Even with the limited testing, you might identify a serial rapist."

"Great. We learn a predator has been running free for fifteen years and that we might have caught him if we'd acted sooner. The governor's never going to let the public hear about it, not without a lot of spin. He never thought testing was a priority. He still doesn't, not really." She forced a smile. "I've vented enough. Thanks for your patience."

"Wait. I get that testing rape kits is a low priority. What I don't understand is how you identified Daniel as a suspect in Sheila's case."

"Because Sheila identified him from physical characteristics, a DNA comparison wasn't used to identify him as a suspect. Because Daniel's DNA wasn't in the perpetrator database, we wouldn't have matched her rape kit data to him, even if we had tested it. After the police arrested him, we tested his DNA sample against the semen and skin taken from Sheila at the hospital. The test confirmed he was the donor of the DNA collected in her rape kit, but it wasn't a priority. Not that it matters. Daniel Lockhart is free and Sheila Fanning is under arrest."

"One last thing. Daniel Lockhart is going to file a motion to have his DNA records expunged. How complicated is that on your end?"

"Given that I've never processed an expungement order, I can't say for sure. Technically, removing a file isn't complicated, but our ancient technology and quirky data structures make it challenging. I'm guessing we can do it in-house, but I'd prefer to wait until we load the rape kit data before messing with it just to be sure we don't corrupt anything trying to remove his information. Anything else?"

"No. Thank you, Nora."

With the call ended, I retreated to the small garden at the back of the house. I brushed leaves off a chair and dropped into it. Spring hadn't come to this little patch of nature and most everything was brown, dormant, and sad-looking. It suited me.

I was too tired to read and not tired enough to sleep. With my mind free to wander, my thoughts turned to Sheila. I didn't have to imagine being assaulted or the humiliation that came from being probed and swabbed by nurses and questioned by the police. I'd had that experience when I was a college freshman after a campus cop found me partially dressed in a park. A few weeks later, after I had gotten over the worst of the trauma and humiliation, the news that the boy who had drugged and raped me had impregnated me traumatized me again. My parents all but disowned me. What I couldn't fathom was being arrested and threatened with prison time.

Harper sat down next to me and, to my surprise, dropped a box of tissues on the table.

"You come out here when you're sad," she said. "I'm never certain what you're sad about, but I know how it feels. Sometimes it's good to give into it, but I don't like to see you crying."

I mopped my eyes with a tissue. "For the record, I wasn't crying." I blew my nose. "God, your mother is a mess. I'm surprised you haven't sued me or asked to have me committed."

Harper leaned over and gave me a peck on the cheek. "It's not like I have any place I can go and you still pay the bills."

I laughed, relieved my daughter still loved me, even if tinged with a heavy dose of pragmatism.

"I wouldn't want your job. Innocent people go to jail and guilty ones get off. You get blamed, no matter what. That sucks."

"It's not always like that. Today…well, sometimes, a jury has a hard time locking up someone they know. Rape cases are difficult because it can look like a he-said she-said situation. I believe Daniel Lockhart assaulted Sheila Fanning, but I had to prove it. For a lot of reasons, I didn't. I could live with the verdict if she hadn't been arrested. I just don't understand the meanness of the people who made that decision."

Harper patted my hand, and we enjoyed a silent moment among the sleeping plants, all that needed saying being communicated by touches and glances.

"I need to tell you something," she said, breaking the silence, "and I don't want you to get mad."

"That's not usually a comforting introduction to a conversation between mother and daughter, so just say it, and let's see what happens."

"I'm planning on skipping school tomorrow with some friends to attend a protest against Sheila's arrest. Some college kids are arranging it and I want to go. You could come with me…"

"I don't want you in the street with a bunch of crazy people…" She started to leave, but I pulled her back to her seat. "I'm sorry. That wasn't me saying no, just your mother's knee-jerk fear bubbling to the surface. I can't join you because of work and because I don't see how demonstrating will change anything. Besides, no one would want me there if I did. Are you sure you want to do this?"

"You don't believe in a woman's right to choose? Do you think the government should tell me what to do with my body? I mean, Sheila didn't want to have sex with Mr. Lockhart, no matter what the jury thought. Why should she have to have his baby, raise it, look at it only to be reminded of being attacked?"

Harper's questions struck me as calculated, resembling what a lawyer might ask a jury in a closing argument. "She shouldn't."

"You know you were just four years older than me when you got pregnant?"

I looked at her, a cold sweat beading on my back. "Don't do this, Harper."

"Do what? Say out loud what is obvious? Unlike most of the kids I go to school with, my mother has never been married. There aren't any pictures of anyone who could pass as my father, no mention of him or his family or even what he looked like. You never say I have his eyes, his chin, his this or that. I used to tell kids at school my father died before I was born while on a secret mission, but the lie only lasted until sex ed. There are only a few plausible explanations, but the ones that make the most sense are you either don't know who my father was, or you just had a one-night stand and didn't love him. That sucks, of course, but it is what it is. And if I'm right, you had to consider the same options Sheila did. Only you had a choice. As of today, I don't."

"Please, sweetie…"

"I don't want to know the details of what happened to you, not now if ever, because it happened to me, too. If I think too much about it, I realize I shouldn't exist at all, so I don't. But we've survived, and that's enough." Tears streamed down her face. "What gets me through the dark moments is I know you love me because I'm here. Sometimes, I wonder what it would have been like to have a normal family with a father and brothers and sisters, but some of my friends wish they didn't. So, this is who we are. Let's not pretend to be something else." She handed me a tissue and mopped her eyes with another. "I'll be careful tomorrow. I promise."

I wiped my eyes and nose. "When did you get so smart and so brave?" I caressed her cheek. "Watch out for tear gas and if the crowd stampedes, stand in a doorway to protect yourself. And don't get too close to the crazies because they'll do something stupid, and you'll get drawn into it. And—"

"Stop worrying about me. I'll be careful. You'll have to write me a note saying I missed school because I was sick."

I glared at her, which she answered with an impish grin. "It didn't hurt to try."

Harper stood, announced she had to work on her poster, and headed inside.

I continued to stare at the dormant and dead foliage. The day had been filled with monumental events, the most important of which was my daughter had deduced the primary elements of my so-called secret. While the details hadn't been fully revealed, I had tacitly acknowledged I'd had a choice to make and considered both alternatives.

But it was the details that mattered. It was the details that had imprisoned me and still did. So while Harper knew instinctively that I had considered ending her life, the revelation alone couldn't liberate or unburden me. She said she didn't want to know what happened to me, and the truth was, I didn't want to tell her.

•　　　•　　　•

It was just after eight in the evening when a hand on my shoulder startled me from a deep sleep. I cleared my head to see Harper hovering over me, holding my cell phone. "It has been buzzing non-stop," she said. "Someone named Liz."

"Hey, Liz," I said, trying to hide the sleep from my voice. "What's happening?"

"You need to go to the courthouse. Sheila is being arraigned. I think the attorney general is trying to get her remanded while no one is paying attention. She's got a public defender, but I think you need to be there."

"To do what?" I said sharply.

"You know what lawyers do. Keep her out of jail. What's wrong with you?"

"Sorry. I'm leaving right now. Ten minutes."

"I'm going with you," said Harper, her tone making it clear she wasn't asking permission.

Liz met us at the courtroom door. "Sheila's case will be called shortly. Her mother is waiting inside." She cocked her head, a question written on her face. "Harper? When did you get so grown up?"

We stepped inside the courtroom and watched as the day's criminals were formally charged, entered a plea, and considered for bail. Most had priors and weren't trustworthy enough to be let free. Sheila's case was called and a lawyer from the attorney general's office came forward. A young woman who claimed to represent Sheila quickly joined him. Sheila stood before the bench, her hands cuffed at her waist.

"What's going on?" asked Harper.

"This procedure is called an arraignment. The magistrate will read the charges against her unless she waives the reading, then she'll be asked if she understands the implications of what she's being charged with, and then she'll be asked to enter a plea."

"It isn't fair," said Harper. "Can't you help her?"

"I don't represent her," I said lamely. "The presiding judge is Judge Rennick. He's always been fair when it comes to bail."

"May it please the court, Justin Myers, for the state…"

The judge held up his hand. "Please remove the cuffs from this woman immediately," he said wearily, "and let's dispense with the formality. Who represents the accused?"

The young woman stepped forward. "Beverly Lake public defender for Ms. …she glanced at a sheet of paper…Ms. Fanning. We waive the reading of the charges and plead not guilty. I am asking for her release without bond."

"That's Mrs. Fanning," said the judge. He turned to the prosecutor. "Okay, Mr. Myers. Objections?"

"We believe the accused is a flight risk, your honor. She has limited ties to the community…"

Harper looked at me, expectations and demands in her eyes.

To my surprise, I stood. "May I have a word with Ms. Lake?"

The judge sighed. "Why not? Dinner is already cold. And you are?"

"Ashley Corbin, State Attorney."

"You want to speak with the defendant's counsel? I'm confused, which at this hour isn't surprising, but why don't you just say your piece and we'll all hear it together?"

I joined the defendant and the other lawyers in front of the bench. "I worked with Sheila for months on her rape trial. She is a determined and honest person. I think we can all agree she isn't likely to commit the crime she's accused of again. She doesn't represent a threat to the community or herself. As for being a flight risk, in my judgment, that's very unlikely."

The judge leaned back in his chair, turning from me back to Justin Meyers and then back to me again. He took off his reading glasses and shook his head. "Now this is a first. A prosecutor from the AG's Office and another from the state attorney's office opposing each other in open court. Do you guys ever talk to each other, you know, before you enter my courtroom?"

I stepped forward. "I'm not speaking in my capacity as a prosecutor, but—"

The judge raised his hand. "Save it, Ms. Corbin. I don't care what your capacity is, but I take your opinion seriously." He looked at Sheila. "I don't know the details of your case, but I don't see the point of adding to your misery by remanding you and locking you up with the community's most unsavory. Please go home and don't leave the area without checking with the state attorney's office first. You'll surrender your passport if you have one, and the sheriff will install a tracking device on your ankle. Agreed?"

With the wrap of a gavel, the gathering before the bench dispersed, and the next accused criminal was paraded to the front of the courtroom. I was halfway to the door when Sheila's mother approached and took my hands.

"Thank you," she said. "I can go home knowing she's not in jail. When will they release her?" she asked.

"They have to process her out of the system and fit her for a tracking device. The police station is just across the street. You can meet her there. I'll go with you if you'd like."

She smiled at Harper. "This is your daughter? Such a pretty girl."

Martin joined us. "Do you know what you've done?" he asked in a parental tone that usually preceded a scolding. But after a momentary icy stare, a smirk grew on his face.

"The right thing?" said Liz, answering the rhetorical question with one of her own.

"It feels that way," he said, "at least for now."

•   •   •

I led Liz, Helena, and Harper across the street to the police administration building. Families of the recently paroled and others with police business packed the lobby. Many shielded their faces or sat with their head in their hands. This was not the place to be recognized. The desk sergeant informed us it would take a few minutes to finish Sheila's processing and suggested we wait on the benches outside.

When we stepped outside, I noticed a man hovering in the shadows. He shuffled forward so the light from the streetlamp would illuminate his upper torso, all the while keeping his head down. Slowly, with a dramatic flair that was a commentary on his self-importance, he raised his eyes, revealing the face of Daniel Lockhart, smirk and all.

I told the others to sit tight and approached him. "What the hell do you want?"

"Just out for a stroll, counselor. Good to be a free man. Anyway, you did better tonight than this morning. Not sure if Sheila will be safer out of jail than in. When you kill babies, no one likes you much."

"Rapists aren't exactly everyone's favorite, especially in prison. So, tell me what you want and then crawl back into the hole you crawled out of."

He looked at Harper. "She's a sweet-looking thing. Such a dangerous world we live in today."

I was no physical match for Daniel but hearing Harper's name filled me with adrenaline. I bolted towards him and slammed my hands into his chest. He stumbled backward and gawked at me in disbelief.

"You don't know me," I said, my voice sounding unfamiliar and animal-like, "so I'll assume you're either stupid or foolish or both. Either way, when you threatened my child, you crossed a line that you'll regret."

I turned to leave, but Daniel recovered and grabbed my arm. "What I want is your cooperation. What I want is for you to accept that the jury found me innocent and for you to stop calling me names. Agree to the expungement motion I filed and no harm will come to you or anyone you love. Stop messing with me, and I'll disappear. Keep doing what you're doing and I won't care what lines I cross."

Daniel retreated into the shadows and was gone. A moment later, Helena appeared. "Was that Daniel Lockhart? What the hell did he want?"

"He's afraid of something," I said, almost to myself. "He's afraid I'm going to find out what it is." I looked at Helena. "He should be."

CHAPTER EIGHT

I spent a restless night rehashing the trial and its aftermath. When I slept, I saw Daniel leering at Harper, grabbing her. She cried out for me, but no matter how hard I ran, I couldn't reach her. The terror of Daniel preying on my daughter returned in various forms until I finally just stayed awake.

I made coffee and then read an invitation from Martin to join him on Blind Eye, an encrypted messaging service. I spent a few minutes loading the app on my phone and verifying my identity. Moments later, I received a confirmation message and, to my surprise, a welcoming text from Martin reminding me to purchase a burner phone and text him the number using the Blind Eye app.

A few days ago, I might have found the effort to hide conversations from state officials who were supposed to be my colleagues—not to mention superiors—to be evidence of paranoia, but today it seemed prudent.

With my communications secured, I sipped coffee and searched the internet for news about the protest march Harper was determined to attend. Overnight, the demonstration had been the subject of intense legal maneuvering. The attorney general moved to block a permit for the rally, citing public safety concerns. The protest organizers and the ACLU filed a motion with a federal magistrate and won an injunction blocking the order to cancel the event.

One pundit wrote that the state feared more people would protest Sheila Fanning's arrest—and, by extension, the abortion law—than support it. The visuals of Main Street being clogged with young people and average folks vehemently disagreeing with the governor's policy were certain to be national news and politically damaging to the governor's rumored presidential ambitions. Another wrote that emotions were high and that violent clashes among demonstrators and police were possible.

I had hoped Harper would inform me she'd changed her mind, but then she appeared wearing a T-shirt on which she had drawn Sheila's likeness and printed the words, FREE SHEILA! On the back were the words, ABORT GOVERNOR ADAMS! Even with the limitations of drawing on cloth with markers and pens, the image and text made quite a statement.

"No confusion about whose side you're on," I quipped. "Will you be warm enough? I mean, it's chilly this morning."

"I'll be fine. I'll wear it over a black long-sleeved shirt."

I nodded my approval. "You should eat something in case you're arrested."

Uncertainty quickly replaced the confidence that had been burning in Harper's eyes. "Protesting isn't against the law," she said meekly.

"Someone throws a rock or hits a cop or does something stupid and the police will round up everyone they can grab. I'm not trying to dissuade you from going, but you need to be aware of your surroundings and the mood of the police."

She scowled at me. "Why do the cops have to be so mean? We have the right to say what we think."

"Theoretically, but less so recently. I'm just asking that you be careful and understand what's going on around you. Now, how about pancakes and bacon?"

•　　　•　　　•

With breakfast accomplished and my cautionary instructions repeated a dozen times, we left the house. I said goodbye to her a few blocks from the courthouse, waiting until she was out of sight before bracing myself with my hands on my knees. I wanted to go after her, to protect her. She was my child, my baby, and here she was, challenging the authority of the state, the governor, and the legal system. I took several deep breaths before straightening up and continuing to my office.

I entered the courthouse, resigned to having no control over how the day would unfold for either Harper or me. Inserting myself in Sheila's arraignment hearing was certain to draw the ire of the attorney general. What I didn't know was when the haranguing would start and when I would learn the consequences of my actions.

I sat at my desk scrolling through emails without reading them, then made a half-hearted attempt to learn what I could about motions for expungement. Mostly, I thought about Harper and how soon she would be off the street and back in the safety of our home.

An obnoxiously demanding ring coming from my desk phone pulled me from my computer screen. I muttered the words, "Leave me alone," and was pleased that, as if in compliance with my directive, the ringing stopped. But a flashing light indicated the caller had been put on hold.

Lisa Calloway, the front office receptionist, appeared at my door and shot me her best peeved look.

"I don't forward calls to you so you can ignore them," she said in a scolding tone. "Anyway, this one you'll want to take. The lady on the line says she's Rose Compton and was the forewoman on the jury that acquitted Daniel Lockhart. She'd like to speak with you about the case."

Interviewing jurors after a trial is controversial and, in some jurisdictions, illegal. Judge Tawney had instructed the jurors they had no obligation to speak with anyone and, under no circumstances should they discuss the deliberations of the jury with anyone. I was certain I was already on the attorney general's shit list and it would be prudent to avoid pissing off a judge who could hold me in contempt. I looked at the blinking light, shrugged, then picked up the phone.

"This is Ashley Corbin. How can I help you?"

"I need to talk to you. What happened to that girl was a travesty. You gotta come here because I don't have a cat sitter, and Sparky can't be trusted to be in the house alone. He got upset when I was gone for jury duty because his regular sitter got sick and he didn't like the new one, so he stopped using his kitty box. That's why I'm not protesting—that and I have asthma. I guess you didn't need to hear all that, but what you need to know is what went down in that jury room and see if you can fix it."

"Rose? May I call you Rose?"

"Of course, you can call me Rose. That's my name."

"The judge strongly advised you against talking about what went on in the jury room. Do you remember?"

"The judge was a sourpuss and full of beans." She coughed and then cleared the phlegm from her throat. "Do you want to talk to me or not?"

I did. I took down the address and told her I'd be there in thirty minutes.

Before I left the office, I checked my cell phone for messages. I was certain I wouldn't hear from Harper until the demonstration ended, but I checked anyway. As I was about to leave, Martin sent me a message reminding me that important communications should be made via encrypted text or burner phones. In a separate message, he informed me that Judge Tawney had scheduled a hearing on the expungement motion for three o'clock in his chambers and that the attorney general was furious that I had inserted myself into Sheila's arraignment hearing. The salient part of the message was in all caps: EXPECT A SHITSTORM WHEN THAT NEWS HITS THE GOVERNOR'S OFFICE.

The prospect that I may have pissed off both the attorney general and the governor amused me in a childish way. That I might later add Judge Tawney and Phillip Dunlevy to the list was also satisfying. For now, the task was to find out what had happened in the jury room that Rose thought I needed to fix.

•　　•　　•

Rose Compton lived in Brightwood. Brightwood was a neighborhood of small homes built during World War II that provided inexpensive housing for a collection of military and civilian families assigned to a logistics and resource planning task force. The Village of Freeman's Gate wasn't strategically located from a military or war perspective and seemed an odd place to locate a task force of any kind. The scuttlebutt was that the group was working with the engineering department of the state university on a secret project and had been located in the Village for security reasons. Whatever the origin of the neighborhood was, both locals and realtors consider it low-income, branding those living there as lower class or worse.

Like all homes in Brightwood, Rose's home was a small brick rambler with a picture window on the left side of the entry door and a double sliding window to the right. The houses occupied a small lot, allowing for a small tree, a few azaleas, or maybe a small patch of flowers.

Before I reached the entry steps, the front door opened, revealing a woman dressed in a bathrobe and slippers and holding a coffee mug. A cigarette dangled from her lips. To my relief, she exhaled a cloud of smoke and dropped the butt into her cup before I got within range of her breath.

"Sorry about the cigarette. I've quit a hundred times, but it doesn't last. I'm sure it'll be the death of me. Probably not the thing for a woman with asthma to be doing, but it is what it is."

"Thank you for seeing me," I said.

She turned and headed inside, talking as she walked. "Shut the door behind you. Don't want Sparky getting loose."

I followed her and quickly shut the door.

"With what happened to that young woman, I can't sleep at night. Maybe talking to you won't fix it, but someone needs to know." She turned and faced me. "Just made a fresh pot of coffee. How do you take it?"

I hesitated, then realized that the prejudices I grew up with about the neighborhood were coloring my opinion of Rose and, to my shame, even her coffee.

"I would love some. Black is fine."

I took a seat at a small kitchen table. With the coffee served, she joined me. Before the conversation started, a large Siamese cat gracefully alighted on the table, flopped down between us, and started purring.

"Good morning, Sparky," I said, then looked at Rose, who was beaming at me. "He's a handsome boy."

"I can move him if you like."

I shook my head. "This is his house."

She rubbed his ears and under his chin. "It is. Nice of you to say so. I don't know how I'd manage without him. You know, my husband…" She pursed her lips. "You didn't come here to listen to the sad whining of a lonely old cat woman. Nothing like what that poor Sheila Fanning girl has had to endure."

"Before you get started, you should know it's probably improper for me to be here and you might get in trouble for speaking to me." I took a sip of coffee. "That's very good."

"It's the cinnamon I add before I brew it. Some folks don't take to it, but I think it makes the coffee a tad sweeter. I've got diabetes so I can't add a lot of sugar and the fake stuff makes me sick."

"Very nice," I said. I patted Sparky lightly, and he rolled on his back and looked at me upside down.

"Talking to you might be improper," said Rose, "but not as improper as the shit that went on at that trial."

"So, tell me about the jury, how you viewed the evidence, what made you vote to acquit Daniel Lockhart. If I screwed up, please just say so. Knowing what mistakes I made can help me get better."

"Oh, no. You did fine. Really." She patted my hand, coughed, and cleared her throat. "What's stuck in my craw is that ten of us were convinced she was raped. All this malarky about her enjoying herself was that lawyer blowing smoke. The guys on the jury first voted to convict, but two jurors kept asking about whether she liked the sex— and they asked a bit too much."

"The same two?"

Rose nodded. "Yup. They kept saying it over and over, and then some men started having doubts. After that, some women thought Sheila had flirted with Mr. Lockhart and that no man could resist that kind of teasing. Little by little, you could see Daniel getting more support. A few of us wanted to discuss facts, but the two jurors who were pushing us to acquit him weren't interested in reviewing the record or the other evidence. It was all about Sheila wanting what she got. It was disgusting."

"Do you remember their names?"

"One of them was Roger. He was the most aggressive. The other was Stacey or Sally—no, it was Denise. I don't remember names so good, but she was always talking about Jesus and abortion, which made no sense until after the trial. They wanted the defendant acquitted and wouldn't shut up about it."

I rubbed Sparky behind the ears. "Were Roger and Denise connected? Did you get the impression they knew each other?"

"They pretended not to, you know, shaking hands and introducing themselves, but you could see they did. I saw them texting during the break. One would type and the other would read. Then they'd switch up. You could see they were exchanging thoughts. That woman juror also referred to the lieutenant governor by her first name, Tanya. I think the other juror, the male, was calling the defendant and his lawyer by their first names. I didn't like it one bit, but I kept my opinions to myself."

"Did any of the other jurors argue for acquittal?"

Rose shrugged. "Not at first, but then the two of them took over the discussion. I was the foreperson and I couldn't get them to shut up. Toward the end, Roger was telling the jurors we had to be absolutely certain, which isn't the same thing as reasonable doubt. Then the woman warned everyone if we didn't agree, there would be a mistrial, and we'd all have to come back and listen to the evidence again. Another lie."

Rose looked at me through tear-filled eyes. "I was the last holdout, but the rest of them wanted to go home. So, I caved because I was worried about Sparky, and we acquitted him. None of us knew about her getting pregnant and the plan to arrest her. I think we were bamboozled. You did a good job with that old codger of a judge, but he was on Daniel's side, and everyone knew it."

"Are you saying it was more likely than not she was raped, but you just weren't sure beyond a reasonable doubt?"

"That's a fair way to put it. Most of us believe he did it, but we couldn't be absolutely sure, so we let him go. Thinking back, I was sure. I was just a coward. Can you make this right?"

The two stubborn jurors during the jury selection process had assured the court they were objective and didn't know the defendant or the victim. Rose had suggested otherwise.

"Daniel Lockhart can't be tried again for the same crime," I said.

The corners of Rose's mouth tightened. "We let her down," she said. "I had one chance to do the right thing, and I let her down."

"Don't do that to yourself. You were asked to decide whether Daniel Lockhart should be locked up for a long time. That's not an easy thing to do."

She looked at me fondly. "When your daughter was a baby, my momma used to take care of her while you were at work. Oh, how she loved that little girl."

For a moment, I was stunned into disbelief. "Eva was your mother? Oh my God, I can't imagine what I would've done without her. I was sorry to hear she died."

"Momma used to tell me how kind you were despite all your troubles. Here you are, a beautiful, smart lawyer trying to help that poor girl. Lots of people let bad things beat 'em down, but you did real good. Funny that you're now trying to make me feel better. Small world."

I thanked Rose for coming forward while offering stale platitudes about doing her civic duty while hoping to hide my disappointment behind social niceties. A hung jury and Sheila would probably not have been charged. Rose had cast the last vote to acquit Daniel Lockhart because her cat was by himself, thereby sealing Sheila's arrest.

Only when I reached my car did I allow myself to indulge my anger and disappointment. I closed the door and screamed an expletive, and then, for a moment, pressed my head against the steering wheel. It wasn't Rose's or Sparky's fault that Roger and Denise were on the jury. I had juror challenges left over. I could have…

I snapped my head up and finished the thought. Planting jurors wasn't foolproof. I could have excluded them. The other jurors could have reported them or simply not voted to acquit. If the grand scheme was to acquit Daniel of rape and then arrest Sheila for an illegal abortion, the plan made little sense. What was the contingency plan if Daniel was convicted or if the jury couldn't reach a verdict?

The whole point of trying Daniel Lockhart was to have a reason to indict and arrest Sheila Fanning. By punishing and humiliating her, the authorities hoped to deter other women and doctors from using the rape exception. The governor and his minions were on a mission for power over women's bodies, a mission cloaked in self-righteousness and divine inspiration. So, why such a risky plan?

With the question begging for an answer that wasn't forthcoming, I was no longer straddling the fence or waiting for someone else to save her. I was Alice, staring at a rabbit daring me to follow him. Even knowing that chasing rabbits was a bad idea, I had arrived at the rabbit hole and was eager to get started.

CHAPTER NINE

I checked my phone, but Harper hadn't texted me. Instead, I found an encrypted text from Martin, urging me to click on a link to a CNN story. I followed the instructions and stared at the image of my only child being interviewed by an adult male reporter on national news, then replayed the clip with the volume up high. My heart swelled with pride as she spoke clearly and calmly about why she was protesting, expressing herself beyond her years. The video closed with a brief observation from the reporter:

"That was Harper Corbin, daughter of the prosecutor who just yesterday lost the rape trial of Sheila Fanning. We can only wonder if the younger Corbin shares her view of the governor with her mother."

The video closed with a picture of Harper's shirt and the words: ABORT GOVERNOR ADAMS.

The commentary provoked a chuckle and a loud, "Oh my God." I was certain Martin was wondering how Harper's interview fit in with the concept of keeping a low profile, but whatever the consequences, the interview left me giddy.

I played it several more times before turning my attention to a missed call from Eric Graham, a good friend and one of a few cops on the force whom I trusted. My first thought was about Harper, and it set my heart pounding. He picked up right away.

"Counselor," he said in his deep monotone voice only friends would recognize as his cheerful voice.

"Is Harper okay?"

"She is. I took her home and other than a bit of a lingering cough…"

"Wait. What happened?"

"You don't know? The state troopers broke the protest up with tear gas. I found Harper and got her away from the crowd. I got her some eyewash at the drugstore and took her home. She's okay, but she asked me not to tell you because of how you get."

"Oh my God, is she…What do you mean, how I get?"

"She's fine but listen to me. She's excited. She's feeling empowered. You know she was on CNN? Watching her speak her mind kind of reminded me of her mother. She doesn't want to be coddled, so let her call you and tell you what she wants you to know."

"You're sure she's okay?"

"She will be. Just let her deal with it herself."

"How did you get to be so smart about mothering kids?"

He grunted. "I raised two girls of my own and made lots of mistakes."

With my fears addressed, I turned to a lingering question. "What were you doing at the demonstration?"

"The sheriff told us the demonstration was to be handled by state troopers sent by the governor's office. The chatter at the police station was that the troopers had been told to push hard on the protestors and keep the governor's supporters safe. More to the point, a lot of them didn't have to be told. The world saw Harper's T-shirt on TV. A lot of young girls were there carrying signs that weren't flattering to the governor. If I were a trooper looking for points from the boss, I'd go after one of them. Picking on kids just doesn't sit well with me. Anyway, she's at home nursing her eyes and very proud of herself."

"You are a sweet man, especially for a cop. I can't thank you enough."

"Okay, let's not get all sappy, because there is some bad news as well. Late last night, I was called to a domestic dispute that turned out to be at Sheila's apartment. By the time we got on the scene, Sheila had taken a punch to the face from her husband, Quinton. I read him the riot act while he blubbered and cried about how sorry he was. Then I told Sheila if she filed a complaint, I could get a restraining order against him. She declined and said the usual crap about the fight being her fault, how it was just a misunderstanding, and that Quinn was a good person. He isn't. He'll hit her again. She's not safe. I can't protect her if she won't let me."

I heard the frustration in Eric's voice, a feeling I shared.

"Did anything provoke him?"

"She told me he'd been looking at his computer and drinking, then just got enraged. I checked it and it was full of messages claiming Sheila had aborted his child and videos showing her having sex with other men. The latter were AI-generated, but they looked real. There was also a social media post from Tanya Cobb accusing Sheila of being a liar, a loose woman, and a baby killer. Daniel Lockhart was posting about how she'd come on to him, tempted him. Then he accused her of murdering *his* son. In a separate post, directed at Quinton, he asserted she'd killed Quinton's son."

"If you're drinking and predisposed to think your wife is cheating on you, that will get you hot."

"Daniel and Tanya were taunting Quinn. It's all crap, of course, but people believe it. What pisses me off is that Sheila isn't safe in her own home and Daniel Lockhart is walking free. How does that happen?"

The snarky response was that her prosecutor lost the case, but the truth was something else.

"If you have time to meet me at the Shade Tree Café, I might be able to answer that question."

•   •   •

I had to fight the impulse to run home to mother my only child, who, of course, wasn't exactly a child despite my effort to imagine her that way. Eric was right about leaving her be, but that didn't make the decision easy for me.

On the way to meet Eric, I stopped at a filling station to buy a burner phone. The attendant wasn't young and didn't have acne, but he was appropriately indifferent, yet knowledgeable and helpful. He reached under the counter and retrieved a box. "This one will allow you to text and surf the web. It comes with a SIM that you have to validate online with a credit card. Kind of defeats the purpose when you think about it. I can sell you a preloaded SIM for sixty dollars. When you run out of minutes, come back and I'll reload it. All cash."

I looked in my wallet and he laughed. "Nobody carries cash these days. The ATM is behind the chips."

•　　　•　　　•

Old Town is a half-mile-long promenade of shops and restaurants along the eastern shore of the Piney River. The structures were once tobacco and cotton barns that had plagued generations of civic leaders. Civic leaders rejected proposals to tear them down, deeming the project too costly. Developing them was a popular notion, but it was hard to see how the investment would ever provide sufficient return to justify the cost. The handwringing ended when a bright young mayor toured Savannah's River District and saw how to manufacture a tourist venue out of decaying buildings and rubble. His vision culminated in a plaza with a museum and welcoming center, a mall, specialty shops, a park overlooking the Piney River, and, of course, food.

One of my favorite spots was The Shade Tree Café. The coffee menu was extensive, and the pastries would tempt me even if I were a diabetic. To my detriment, the café was within walking distance of my house.

When I arrived, Eric was sitting in a booth in the far corner of the café, tilting his head toward a menu. Wearing a sweater and sporting black reading glasses perched on the end of his nose, he could have been mistaken for an English lit professor. His beard and mustache were whiter than I remembered, the last of the pepper having been replaced with salt. He still had a thick head of long hair, but it, too, was giving up its once dark brown hue.

He glanced up as I slid into the seat opposite him but returned his gaze to the menu. The appearance and departure of brow furrows animated his face and clenched lips.

"How many ways are there to make coffee?" he asked.

I pulled the menu from his hands and set it on the table. "Do you like chocolate?"

When he nodded, I asked, "And whipped cream?"

"Hell yeah."

A waitress approached. "We'll have two large cappuccinos with shaved chocolate and whipped cream." I pointed to Eric's mustache. "Better bring extra napkins."

He laughed. "I bet that cost a month's pay."

"A reason not to get addicted to it," I said. "I can't thank you enough for taking care of Harper. Maybe I'll put you in for cop of the year and get you a commendation to hang on your wall."

Eric looked around the café, then at me. "If you knew me better, you might reconsider."

"What does that mean?"

Eric shook his head. "Long boring story."

"Humor me."

He grimaced. "When I was just out of the academy, I fell into a group of older guys headed up by a homicide detective. I saw things that weren't by the book—guys taking money off drug dealers, some product, that sort of thing. I didn't report it because I was told not to, and even if I wanted to, I didn't know who I could trust. Go along to get along was the rule. But then one of the guys shot an unarmed kid. Predictably, someone put a gun in the kid's hand, and the review board ruled the shooting justified. The detective made sure I knew to keep quiet."

"He threatened you?"

"The way cops do. Nothing overt, but nothing left to doubt either."

"Eric—"

"Let me finish. The mother of that boy loved him and his death all but killed her. Worse, she depended on him for income to support the other kids. I couldn't live with myself. When I tried to report the detective, I was told I could leave the force with a recommendation, or I could be brought up on unspecified charges—planted drugs or money would be my guess—so I left and came here. That was a lifetime ago. I never made detective and gave up trying. To be honest, I was thinking of retiring even before the crazies took over. Now? I can't do this anymore."

"That's…wow. I don't know what to make of it."

"Just an old story.

The coffee arrived and for a moment, the fifty-five-year-old man looked like a wide-eyed kid. "Oh, my."

We sipped and savored for a few minutes. "Hard to believe that's coffee," he said. "I think you should speak with Sheila to see if you can convince her to file charges against her husband."

"I spoke with her mother. Sheila won't file a complaint against Quinn. I want to help her, but—"

"You need to think of something. After I pulled Harper from the demonstrations, she begged me to help Sheila. Her eyes are burning, she can barely breathe, and her first thought is about a woman she doesn't know. Helping Sheila is out of my skill set, but not yours. Harper is going to come around to the same conclusion, and you need to be ready for it. You can give Harper a dozen reasons why you can't, but she isn't going to buy any of them."

"I haven't seen you in months and you're full of parenting advice." I rolled my eyes. "That sounded harsh, and I didn't mean it that way."

Eric stared into his empty cup. "No offense taken. I'm not a fan of abortion but sending a young woman who was raped to prison for having one is unfair and cruel. Torquing her husband into beating her is just sadistic. Sheila doesn't deserve any of this shit."

He looked at me, his face a mask of sadness. "I just don't know what's happened to our town. It seems like yesterday we were doing unto others, loving our neighbors, and getting along, even if we didn't see things the same way. Now, we're gassing kids and screaming words of hate at each other. I don't get it. I don't want to get it. That's not what I signed up for."

"A cop with a heart," I said with a laugh. "It must be the end of days."

"A lawyer with a conscience." Eric shrugged. "Maybe we should both be worried."

I spooned out the thick sludge of chocolate-infused whipped cream from the bottom of my cup and held it up where Eric could see it. "This is the best part," I said, then closed my eyes and savored it.

"I forget how young you are," he said. "Makes me feel old."

"I don't see you that way."

After we finished the coffee, we found ourselves immersed in a comfortable silence. Then, the weariness returned to Eric's face. "So, how did Daniel Lockhart manage to go free?"

"The short—slightly paranoid—version is Daniel had ringers on the jury and a defendant-friendly judge was assigned to the case. But that alone couldn't guarantee that Daniel would be acquitted. I haven't figured it out and maybe never will. Of course, even if I could find some kind of tampering, the state can't appeal a not-guilty verdict, so there's no fixing it."

Eric scraped the bottom of the cup with a spoon. "Doesn't explain how the governor showed up after the trial to announce Sheila's arrest."

"No, it doesn't. Sheila didn't tell me she was pregnant. I doubt she'd tell the attorney general. I mean, why would she? She was bringing charges against Daniel for rape. Yet somehow the AG knew about Sheila's abortion, but how did he find out? And how do you explain he was ready to arrest her almost immediately after the verdict in the rape trial was announced? That takes planning and a cold heart. I know it sounds conspiratorial, but I don't care. If I'm right, some diabolical scheme went down and the perpetrators look to be getting away with it. I can't live with it, but at the moment I can't prove it. It stinks, and it makes me cranky."

Eric thanked me for the coffee, promised to call to check on Harper, and left the café.

I glanced at my phone, hoping to find a message from Harper, but there was nothing. Instead, I texted Martin that Sheila needed to be put in protective custody even if it meant revoking her bail. He responded the attorney general's office had denied his request for protection, probably because letting Quinn beat her up seemed to please the governor's supporters. He closed by saying he'd like to talk to me about a certain young woman and her T-shirt.

I ordered another coffee and watched the news about the demonstration on my phone, then rewatched Harper's interview while reprising my role of proud mother.

The joy was short-lived. A photograph of the Lieutenant Governor, Tanya Cobb, appeared. She was surrounded by supporters and, to my surprise, standing next to acquitted rapist Daniel Lockhart. The anchor offered a few introductory words and then played a clip from an interview with Tanya in which she denied that there were two sides to the abortion issue:

"There is only one moral truth that was given to us by the one true Savior. The laws of man are subservient to the laws of the Maker, and He has demanded that His soldiers fight the battle against the abomination of abortion by any and all means without regard to the secular laws, which, in many cases, have been tinged with evil. Mr. Lockhart and his aborted son are both victims of this heinous crime, and I'm here with him to support his demand for justice."

The anchor then played another clip of Tanya addressing whether the governor was planning to run for president:

"The governor is a man of God who has been directed to do His will. If running for president is what our Savior wants, God will prepare Warren to lead others to His side and stamp out those who fail to heed the true word. Under his leadership, we will become the Christian nation our founders envisioned."

The segment ended with a brief interview with Daniel Lockhart:

"I was singled out for prosecution by a local woke prosecutor. My lawyer presented proof that the sex I had with that woman was consensual and that she initiated it. I only learned after the trial that she killed my son. She murdered an innocent child to hide her adultery. I'm here today to thank the attorney general and the lieutenant governor for expressing their condolences over my loss. I plan to assess my legal rights against the state attorney's office and against the woman who intentionally caused me to endure significant emotional and financial distress."

I sat back in my chair and exhaled slowly. I imagined Harper living in a world built according to Tanya's worldview, a world controlled by an intolerant society following edicts dictated by a single religious dogma. The exercise was sobering and confounding. I wouldn't have entertained such a thought even a week ago or, if I had, I would have dismissed it as some crazy notion inspired by bad sushi.

Yet here I was, surprised by how the place I called home seemed to have morphed overnight into a dystopian state. In this world, Daniel was the victim and had threatened to sue the woman he'd raped.

The most troubling part of this vision of my present reality was it hadn't happened overnight or in the last month or the last year. The transition of the Village of Freeman's Gate from a Waltons-esque small town to an increasingly intolerant community had happened slowly, incrementally, and in plain sight. Looking back, the signs were there: the change in the school board, the attitude toward books, the debates over which history to teach, the arguments over guns, and the fuming about the federal government.

With the loss of civility came the loss of rights. The trend line was such that one day, we would lose our last rights, and they'd be gone forever.

The vexing question was what was I prepared to do about it?

CHAPTER TEN

The walk to the office took me close to the site of the demonstration. I could smell the tear gas and saw protestors headed away from the point of confrontation. Some stopped to pour water into their eyes to douse the burning, while others appeared defeated. What struck me was how young they were. Most were college students. Some were still in high school and too young to vote in the last election.

I could only wonder what these kids thought about their treatment by the government that was sworn to protect them, by adults that had infused them with the American ideal of free speech, the right to assembly, and the right to petition leaders to redress grievances. Of course, these rights had limits, but had these children actually stepped over some imaginary line and become a threat to society? Did they deserve to be gassed and clubbed for expressing an opinion?

After seeing them, I fought the impulse to call Harper, knowing Eric was right. She would call me when she was ready. He had assured me he'd taken care of her. I told myself I had to give her space. But when I reached the courthouse, my resolve weakened. I still had a few hours before I was due in the judge's chambers. My motherly instincts took charge, and I kept walking. I was eager to get home, see my daughter, give her hugs if she wanted them, and for a few precious moments not think about the past, the future, work…none of it.

But wanting to not think about something is the surest way to have your head filled with whatever subject you're avoiding. By the time I stepped inside the house, I was mentally exhausted.

I called out and heard a response from the living room. She looked up at me from the sofa, her eyes red and puffy.

"Don't be mad at me. Please. I'm okay."

"Fine. I won't be mad at you if you promise not to be mad at your mother."

Worry crossed Harper's face. "Why would I be mad at you?"

"It's a long story that I don't have the energy to tell at the moment, but the short version is that I may be fired or suspended because I got involved in Sheila's arraignment. I've violated a court order by speaking to a juror and I'm about to appear before the judge who tried Sheila's rape case and will no doubt say something to piss him off. As to you— that interview was awesome."

Harper bolted from the couch, gave me a high five, and wrapped her arms around me. "Do I need to get a job?"

"I think we can get by on mac and cheese and canned tuna for a while. No one's going to hire someone who looks like the Joker, anyway."

Harper retreated. "That's not funny. I'm certain I'll have self-esteem issues for years to come. That is unless you offer to order carryout from Thai Magic. A double order of curry and Pad Thai. That would go a long way to fixing my emotional distress."

"If I didn't feel sorry for you, I might find being manipulated irritating."

Harper grimaced as her eyes filled with tears. She rubbed them with a damp towel and emitted a moan. "I want this to stop! Make it stop."

"Go to your room, pull the shades and curtains, and lie down. I'll get you a bag of ice. I've got a bit of work to do before I head back to the office for a hearing. You'll be fine in a few hours, and then we'll have dinner."

•   •   •

I brought up Daniel's proposed motion for expungement on my laptop. The first paragraph requested the removal of his DNA data that had been obtained from a sample taken during his arrest from all state databases. The second paragraph requested that any DNA data acquired from Sheila Fanning's crime scene evidence be deleted from the state's forensic database. I understood the logic of the first request, but the second made little sense.

At the confrontation in front of the police station, Daniel made it clear that the motion was important enough to threaten me and Harper. That alone was sufficient reason to object to the motion. But importantly, something about his DNA record worried him, and I wanted to know what it was.

I drafted two responses. One simply stated that the state didn't object. The other was an equally terse objection and a request for a hearing before a judge not involved in Daniel's rape trial. The latter element of the response would likely piss off Judge Tawney. No longer caring about whose feathers I ruffled, I signed both, put them in a folder, and turned my thoughts back to Sheila.

I was conditioned to think like a prosecutor and had to force myself into considering Sheila's predicament from the point of view of her defense counsel. Once in that mode, ideas flooded my mind. The one that stuck was simple and satisfying. The sticking point was that I would need someone else to implement it.

I spent an hour outlining a complaint and then called Liz. When I asked if she knew either of the lawyers representing Sheila and the doctor who'd performed her abortion, she was immediately suspicious.

"Why would a prosecutor be asking a women's rights advocate about defense lawyers?"

"Probably because she shouldn't be asking anyone and certainly can't do it on her own. I have an idea that might help Sheila, but I need an off-the-record meeting with one or both of them today after four."

"I'll text you," she said and hung up.

Five minutes later, Liz confirmed the meeting, with the admonition, "This better be good."

It was.

•   •   •

I opened the blister pack and retrieved my new phone. With the SIM card inserted, I keyed the phone number into an encrypted text and sent it to Martin. I had joined criminals and paranoid folks who were determined to hide from curious and otherwise intrusive authorities. I connected the phone to its charger and then checked on Harper before heading to the state attorney's office in the courthouse.

I had walked through those doors hundreds of times over the years, but today, it felt different. As I cleared the reception desk, I sensed that my connection to the office had changed. Yesterday morning, I left the office for the courtroom a true believer, a soldier in the army of justice and equity, and all the other bullshit that shaped my view of the law as an institution. Today, I returned to my church without my faith, and the feeling saddened me.

Martin was close on my heels. He followed me into my office, shut the door, and pulled a chair in front of my desk.

To my surprise, he smirked. "I've got to hand it to you. You've raised your daughter to be a lot like you. She's angered lots of people in a short time. Probably a record for someone her age. She's getting some pretty nasty hate on social media. I recall saying something about not drawing attention to yourself, but maybe I only thought I did."

"I don't recall you saying anything like that. But yeah. Getting under people's skin is a skill learned when I was younger, and it appears I've passed it on in my genes. So, are you one of the angry ones or just indifferent?"

"Me? Hell no. Harper's T-shirt was classic. When that video circulated in the office, it took everything in me not to applaud right then and there. Not everyone here enjoyed it, but it made my day. What have you been up to?"

I folded my arms across my chest, took a deep breath, and let it out slowly. "How long have we been working together?"

"Shit. This can't be something I want to hear."

I leaned forward. "I know you said we should wait things out, fight the battles we can win, and try to make lemonade out of lemons. Waiting, making juice, and picking the right battles are things I just can't do. What I've been doing and what I'm about to do are going to make things hard for you. You need to keep your distance from my inappropriate behavior. If I don't tell you, you have plausible deniability, something every lawyer learns about in their first year of law school."

"You're saying I should throw you under the bus?"

"I'm saying the bus is going to hit me whether you do or don't. You might as well join the winning side, or appear to. Of course, you don't have to look like you're enjoying it."

Martin folded his hands in front of his mouth. "Let's forget the bus and lemon metaphors and get to the have-dones and gonna dos."

"I met with the jury foreman—woman. Apparently, friends of the governor or the lieutenant governor infiltrated the jury. The not-guilty verdict doesn't reflect what most of them believed."

Martin stared at me, then pursed his lips. "Jury tampering? That's a serious charge, but that you learned it from a juror is probably good for a contempt citation. What else?"

"I'm going to object to Daniel's motion for expungement. There was probable cause he raped Sheila. The jury verdict didn't conclude he didn't, but only that I didn't prove it. I'm going to ask for a hearing in which the burden of proof is on Daniel."

"Novel, but more than likely to piss off Judge Tawney even more. Is that it?"

"Just this. The abortion statute creates an exception for rape but doesn't say how that's to be proven. An argument can be made that the rape exception should be treated like an affirmative defense, in which case Sheila would only have to prove it was more likely than not she was raped. The state would then have to prove she wasn't raped beyond a reasonable doubt. With a different judge and jury, the prejudicial evidence would be inadmissible."

Martin raised an eyebrow. "That's creative and would be laudable if we were her defense attorneys. Kind of tricky if I'm the one who is prosecuting her abortion case."

"That's why I'm meeting with her doctor's lawyer this afternoon."

Reading Martin's face is a skill I have yet to acquire. Good lawyers project what they want others to see. But for a moment, he appeared to be angry with me. I'd made it clear I was no longer willing to acquiesce to the whims of the governor and his sycophants. What I sensed was that we had become adversaries, maybe not over goals, but tactics.

He folded his arms across his chest. "You know announcing that she's going to defend the abortion charge will foreclose any opportunity for a plea deal? They'll threaten her with felony abortion and years in jail. She won't take the risk, or she shouldn't."

"If the doctor who performed the abortion helps fund her defense, she might take the chance on an acquittal. Besides, the optics of the state bashing Sheila after defending her might get the state to back down."

I had referred to the "state" but we both knew in the current context, the state was a euphemism for the State Attorney and, therefore, Martin.

"And just for fun, there's the option of Sheila suing Daniel for damages. Kind of like OJ was after he was acquitted. To be honest, looking at her case from the defense side has given me a whole different perspective."

Martin stood and looked at me coldly. "Enjoy the view while you can. You and I both know this won't have a happy ending."

"Yeah, well, I'm not happy now."

•   •   •

Phillip Dunlevy was waiting for me outside the entrance to the state attorney's office. "We'll be meeting with Judge Tawney. He's using a conference room on the first floor as his chambers."

He handed me a copy of the expungement motion. The motion was concise and direct.

"All data relating to (1) the taking of DNA from Daniel Lockhart, to the DNA sample itself, and Daniel Lockhart's identifying information associated with said sample, and (2) all DNA derived from the person of Sheila Fanning, her clothing, and the place of the consensual sexual activity between her and Daniel Lockhart shall be permanently and irretrievably deleted on an expedited basis from all computers, computer databases, and electronic devices owned, controlled, or used by the state and in any communications between and among law enforcement personnel and between and among forensic personnel."

I handed the motion back to him. "Is your client worried about something?" I asked.

"Just that the government shouldn't have information about him it doesn't need. My opinion—one that is shared by the ACLU—is that taking his DNA before convicting him of a crime violated his Fourth Amendment rights. Now that he's acquitted, he wants the violation cleaned up. Any objections?"

"A few. Daniel threatened me last night. Really pissed me off, so I'm teetering. He confirmed my view that your client is a dangerous man and should be in prison. I'm also sensing he's afraid of something. Any idea what that might be?"

Phillip motioned with his head. "The sting of defeat is best cured by moving on. Let's make nice and make this quick."

When we arrived, Judge Tawney was sitting at the head of a long table, his hands folded in front of him. Time and bad habits had taken a toll on the judge, leaving him with large jowls, drooping eyelids, and dark puffy circles under his eyes. Age spots of varying hues of brown painted on a canvas of sallow skin, and red lines from years of negotiating over glasses of bourbon crisscrossed his cheeks. Collectively, these features made it impossible to know whether he'd been a handsome man in his early days. Whatever his past, he'd evolved into a curmudgeon with a big ego and bullying nature.

We took our seats on opposite sides of the judge. Phillip spoke, but the judge cut him off, then turned his yellowing eyes on me. He didn't smile, or if he did, I couldn't tell.

"Do you have children?"

"Yes, your honor."

"And what does your husband do while you're playing lawyer?"

"I'm not married."

Phillip offered his motion to the judge. "Your honor…"

Judge Tawney's eyes remained focused on me. "Interesting that you're a single mother. Did it help to have something in common with the woman you defended?"

"I'm sorry…"

"I just mean each of you engaged in a dalliance and got in trouble for it. Obviously, you accepted responsibility."

The judge took the motion from Phillip's hand and perused it.

"You are both in agreement with expunging Daniel's DNA records?"

Phillip nodded. "Yes, your honor."

The judge turned his gaze to me. "Must be hard losing a case involving a woman about your age. The jury might have reacted differently if a man had defended her."

"Well, when the jury hears prejudicial testimony, it probably doesn't matter what gender the prosecutor is."

"Let's not re-litigate the trial," said Phillip, before forcing a laugh. "If you'll issue an order, I will serve it on the attorney general and we can get the process started."

My verbal bullet hit home.

"Be careful what you say to a judge, Miss Corbin. Contempt is a very serious charge that could have implications for your license to practice."

I'm sure my eyes conveyed my disdain, but I knew I wouldn't achieve anything sparring with him.

"For the record, the state objects to the motion filed by Mr. Dunlevy. It is overly broad and vague. More importantly, it fails to state the legal principle that supports the requested remedial action. Daniel's DNA sample was taken pursuant to state law that authorizes sampling of those arrested for specified crimes based on a determination that there is sufficient evidence to indicate a crime was committed by the accused. The jury verdict meant that there wasn't sufficient evidence to meet the reasonable doubt standard, not that the police lacked probable cause to take a sample for testing his DNA. At most, the defendant is entitled to a hearing to determine whether it is more likely than not that he didn't rape Sheila Fanning. As to the second enumerated relief, the evidence taken from Sheila Fanning and the crime scene didn't violate any of Daniel Lockhart's constitutional rights because the evidence so obtained wasn't a search of his person or property."

"You want to try the case again?" said Dunlevy.

"I want a hearing before an impartial fact finder," I said calmly, "and not a jury that has been corrupted by political meddling."

The judge glared at me. "Tell me now if you've spoken to a member of the jury."

I stared back at him, my lips pursed into a subtle smile. "Before you go down that path, your honor, do you really want to excite the media circus by arresting both the victim of rape and her prosecutor amid rumors of jury tampering? That can't look good for the state or the court."

Judge Tawney's chicken-white facial skin took on a pinkish hue. While he fumed, I gathered my papers. "With that, I think we've taken enough of your honor's valuable time. If you'll set a briefing schedule in the next few weeks, I'm sure we can have an objective discussion about Daniel's rights and you can rule on his motion."

"I had hoped the trial taught you something, Miss Corbin," said the judge. "You have picked a fight you can't win and one that you'll regret."

Phillip followed me from the conference room, grabbed my arm, and led me into an empty courtroom. "Do you like playing with fire?"

"No, but I wasn't partial to the suggestion that the prosecutor and victim were both whores, so they were certain to get along. Of course, not something roosters have to worry about. Anyway, I'm going to find out what your guilty client is hiding before his DNA data is purged from the state's databases. Of course, we could save a lot of time if you just tell me."

I moved to leave, but Phillip grabbed me again. "You have absolutely no idea how all this unfolded. I knew that Judge Tawney was going to sit for the trial a month ago. It wasn't some random thing, but a selection the governor's office made with the help of the attorney general. I was also told that he distrusts rape victims, especially young pretty ones, because he thinks they taunt men into a hormonal state that the men can't control and aren't responsible for their actions. Then, add to the mix that the prosecutor was another attractive female, and I knew the judge would likely push the boundaries on what testimony would be admissible. You may think what I did was unethical, but my job was to represent my client zealously. And I did."

"What about the jury? How did you manage that?"

"I didn't…"

"And Sheila Fanning is going to prison."

Phillip shrugged. "Regrettable, but not my client and not my problem."

"Daniel rapes someone else—maybe your wife or daughter or a friend, if you have any. That's not your problem either, but you did your duty as a lawyer, so your conscience is clear. Wait. You don't have one of those either."

Phillip stormed out of the same courtroom where, a day ago, my life had changed. I found myself thrust into an unfamiliar space, where only fools followed the rules, and the goal was not justice but winning.

Sheila Fanning found herself pulled into this realm, and for better or worse, I now had to fight with the tools I had, without the constraints of legal niceties like due process and law and order. I wasn't skilled at this game, and I knew it. But I was getting better at it and it felt good.

CHAPTER ELEVEN

Liz had arranged a meeting at the offices of Hugh Daily, who represented Trisha Palmer, the doctor who performed Sheila's abortion. I was told to wait in a conference room where Beverly Lake, Sheila's public defender, was sitting, drinking coffee, and staring at her phone. She glanced at me, shooting me a knowing smile.

"Liz told me this meeting was your idea," she said. "I wasn't keen on the idea of meeting with the prosecutor's office, but curiosity got the best of me."

"I'm not here in my official capacity as a prosecutor, but in my unofficial capacity as someone who thinks your client got a raw deal. I can't change her situation, but maybe you can."

Hugh arrived with Liz right behind him. I overheard a snippet of their conversation in which he was only joining the meeting because the doctor insisted and was really too busy to entertain some off-the-wall legal strategy. When he took a seat at the head of the table and pointed at me, his expression of annoyance clearly reflected his attitude.

"What are you doing here? What are *we* doing here?"

"Preventing an injustice. Saving a young woman from prison. Sticking it to the attorney general. Pick one. All I ask is that you listen for ten minutes. After that, you can leave."

Hugh nodded. "Fair enough. Make your pitch."

I shared my theory that Sheila and the doctor should enter pleas of not guilty based on her asserting that the rape exception to the abortion statute is an affirmative defense that shifted the burden of proof to the state. "The state would have to prove that she wasn't raped," I said, "a burden I don't think the state can meet. Simultaneously, Sheila could then file a civil complaint against Daniel Lockhart, setting forth a cause of action for assault, the physical, emotional, and financial damages he caused her, and a motion for summary judgment based on the transcript from the rape trial. Similarly, your client could file a complaint alleging loss of reputation and slander."

Hugh raised an eyebrow and laughed. "Well, that's certainly creative. What's in it for my client?"

"If the state can't carry its burden, if Sheila prevails on whether—for the purposes of the abortion statute—she was raped, the state can't charge the doctor who performed the abortion. If Sheila wins, your client wins."

"What's the downside?" asked Beverly.

"The doctor and Sheila would give up the opportunity for a plea deal. The state will ask for the maximum sentence, so any leniency would depend on the judge or jury. Sheila takes the most risk because she might avoid prison with a plea. But the plea deal would require an admission she wasn't raped, foreclosing a suit for damages. The equation is different for the doctor. Admitting to a felony might allow her to avoid prison but could impact her ability to continue practicing medicine."

The room was silent. Even Hugh seemed to have changed his attitude. He smiled at me. "You should switch sides," he said. "Let me talk to my client. I'll get back to you."

"Likewise," offered Beverly.

•   •   •

I called in the order for Thai food and walked home. The streets were empty of demonstrators, but the debris from the confrontation with police and supporters of the governor was everywhere. Placards, water bottles, and even a few spent teargas canisters marked the location of the fiercest battle, the one Harper had probably witnessed before losing her ability to see. That most of the protesters were young gave me an inkling of hope, but the revelations of my meeting with Phillip Dunlevy and Judge Tawney convinced me that the battle to provide Sheila justice wouldn't be won in the streets but, if at all, in the courts.

When I reached home, I felt mentally spent and eager to lose myself in a glass of wine and a bowl of curry. Before I could step inside the house, I was stunned to find the front door open. I often neglected to lock it, but the door was always closed. I called out for Harper, desperately listening for a reply as my heart thumped like a drum in my ears.

After a long second, I heard a weak, hesitant voice respond, "In the kitchen."

As I cleared the foyer, I saw Harper seated at the table, her hands clutching a tissue, fighting back tears. After another step, the face of Daniel Lockhart came into view.

"You have a lovely home and daughter," he said. "I thought it would be nice to talk, to clear the air." He laughed. "It may be too late for Harper. Tear gas is nasty stuff."

"Get out!" I screamed in a voice I didn't recognize.

Daniel arched his eyebrows. "Not a friendly way to address someone who was invited in."

"I'm sorry, Mom," said Harper. "He said he was from your office. His face was blurry…"

"It's okay, sweetie."

I took a seat at the table. "Say what's on your mind and be quick about it before I call the police."

"When we met the other night, I may not have been clear. What I want is for you to mind your own business and get out of my life. I'm actually a fun guy when treated nicely. Harper was nice to me. She even offered me a glass of water. But you have been all over town causing trouble. Phillip told me you didn't approve the expungement motion and that you've been plotting with others to have Sheila sue me. Why would you want to hurt me?"

His voice broke as he posed the question, and for a moment, he looked as if he might cry. The face before me wasn't that of a confident and surly rapist but a broken man, someone tormented by ghosts that lived in the dark shadows of his past. I didn't feel sympathetic but wary. An injured animal was unpredictable, mercurial, and capable of anything.

"I don't want to hurt you, Mr. Lockhart, but there is a process I must follow. The judge determines the merits of your motion, not me. My job is to make sure the judge considers all the issues so the decision is legally correct and serves the public interest. It's not personal. Really, it isn't. I can speak with Phillip…"

I was lying in my best imitation motherly voice in a desperate effort to keep the predator at bay, to protect my child.

Daniel fixed his eyes on Harper.

"I don't think Phillip can be my lawyer anymore," he said. "I can't pay him. Maybe I can represent myself. Besides, I know the Lieutenant Governor, Tanya. She doesn't like you much."

"Well, then I'm going to try harder to be a nicer person," I said, trying to distract him. "A jury of your peers said you were innocent. That's the end of it. No one wants to hurt you. We just need to let the process finish and move on. I think this is more a misunderstanding than anything else."

"That's good," he said. "I don't want to hurt anyone either. You can start by withdrawing your objection to the expungement motion. That would be helpful. I don't have the money to keep fighting you. You don't know this, but I lost my dream house because of this case and that was your fault. So, I'm trying not to be angry with you, but you've got to stop harassing me. If you do, we can both move on. What I'm saying is that I promise to leave you alone if you leave me alone. Simple really." He turned to Harper. "Thank you for your hospitality," then looking at me said, "I can find my way out."

I followed him outside, then stepped in front of him. "Don't you ever come here again. I promise I'll have you prosecuted if you do. Keep in mind it can be a felony to stalk a child. You'll be getting a restraining order soon. Violate that and I'll have you arrested and thrown in prison with guys who don't like child molesters."

He started to speak, but I slammed the door in his face. I could hear him screaming obscenities as I made my way to the kitchen. Harper stared at me for a moment, her jaw clenched and brows furrowed, then turned away. She was taking quick breaths punctuated by the word "shit" and was trembling.

"Hey, sweetie. It's okay. He's gone. He's gone."

"It's not okay!"

I kneeled beside her chair and hugged her. "Sorry," I whispered. "I'm so sorry."

"He said he was from your office, and I let him in…" she managed, before choking on her tears.

I stroked her cheek, then kissed her forehead.

"My eyes were watering, and I couldn't see his face, not until he was inside. I didn't know what he was going to do. Why do guys have to be like that? It's not fair."

"They're not all like that."

"But how do I know? He was my teacher…" Her body shook as she gasped for air. "I thought I'd be brave, but I was just too frightened to do anything."

I brushed the tears from her cheeks, then held her head in my hands. "Look at me. This will never happen again."

She looked at me with doubting eyes. "You can't know that. He could follow me home from school or soccer practice. Just the idea he's watching me makes me feel…icky."

Harper was right. Short of shooting Daniel Lockhart, I made a promise that wasn't in my power to keep.

"How about this? Tomorrow, I'll file a restraining order against him. I will do everything I can to put him in prison where he belongs. It may take some time, but you know how I am when I get pissed about something. Until then, we'll be more careful. Maybe I'll get a door camera and a couple of baseball bats. What we can't do is lock ourselves inside. We still have to live our lives, otherwise, he wins."

"You'll lock him up as soon as you can?"

"I'm working on it as we speak. Once the judge approves the restraining order, he can't come within five hundred feet of you without being arrested." I kissed her forehead. "Can you eat something?"

Harper nodded, then left to wash her face. Alone, I barely stifled a scream, but a loud "damn" still filled the kitchen. I busied myself by reheating the Thai food and setting the table, then made a margarita and downed it.

While I made another, I realized Daniel knew I had suggested that Sheila sue him. Who told him that?

When Harper returned, she insisted we not talk about Daniel or Sheila or the trial. She shared that her eyes didn't hurt as much but were still blurry, that none of her friends had been arrested, and that she was a star on social media. I was pleased to hear my reviews were improving because I helped Sheila get out of jail, but I wasn't happy to learn some blamed me for Sheila being arrested in the first place.

But despite her intentions, Harper was still thinking about Daniel's visit.

"What did he mean about you causing trouble?" she asked.

"I had a wonderful conversation with the jury forewoman, made a lasting impression on a judge hearing his motion for expungement, and pitched the idea of suing him to Sheila's and her doctor's lawyers."

"That's good, right?"

"It felt good. The judge might hold me in contempt of court and lock me up, so there is a downside to being a troublemaker. Daniel thinks I'm picking on him. More to the point, he's afraid of something, something connected to his DNA being in the police database. I'm not sure what, exactly, but he seems obsessed with having me approve his expungement motion."

With a small skirmish over the last of the Pad Thai resolved, Harper said what I was thinking.

"Just his being here frightened me," she said. "I can't imagine what Sheila was feeling."

"If he wanted to hurt you, he wouldn't have come here. He wanted to intimidate me by threatening you."

I had directed my words to Harper, but hearing them out loud fathered a question: How did my objecting to the expungement motion *hurt* him?

"What about Sheila?"

"I want to help her, but in all honesty, there isn't much I can do. I gave her lawyer a few options, but everything costs money she doesn't have. Last night, her husband hit her, but she won't leave. When we're done here, I'll call her and see if I can convince her to find a place to stay that's safe."

Harper shrugged but didn't leave. "Call her now." When I didn't reach for my phone, she brought her arms together across her chest. "I want to hear what she has to say."

I found her number in my contacts list. When she answered, I was quick to speak: "This is Ashley Corbin. I heard what happened and wanted to know if there's anything I can do to help you. If you have questions or if you just want to talk, you can always call me."

When she didn't respond, I quickly added, "Your husband can't be beating you. I can get a protective order or move you to a safe place. I want to help you."

"She can stay with us," said Harper.

I shushed Harper with my hand, then heard sobbing. Sheila tried to speak, but her words were incomprehensible. I told her to breathe and to take her time. A minute passed before she was calm enough to speak clearly.

"My husband believes I had sex with Daniel Lockhart because I wanted to. I tried to tell him it wasn't true, but he repeated what Daniel's attorney said in court. Last night, he asked if the baby I aborted was his. He's so angry he scares me. But I can't file a complaint because he won't be able to get a job. He's not a bad person, not really. Just keep the cops away from him and let me deal with him."

"If he hit you once, he'll do it again. If you file a complaint, I'll do what I can to make certain he doesn't hurt you."

"He's always ashamed when he hurts me. Please don't do anything. It'll just make things worse. I'll take care of Quinn."

Harper moved close. "Do something. Say something."

"The best thing you can do is get away from him. He needs help, and you need to be safe."

Sheila took several deep breaths. "I can't deal with this now. I don't want to go to prison. Pleading guilty to a felony for a lighter sentence will kill my legal career before it even starts. My marriage is a wreck. I have no money, and I can't get a job. All this because a man forced himself on me. Mom wants me to fight back, but what if that just makes things worse? All my options suck. You mean well, but this is not your fight. I'll figure it out on my own."

"I didn't know you'd gotten pregnant," I said.

"I didn't tell Quinn, and I didn't tell you because I thought he'd find out. I'm sorry. Looking back, I should have told you. I have to go."

I put down my phone. Tears filled Harper's eyes and streamed down her cheeks. "This can't be the way the world works," she said, then bolted from the table.

It could and it was.

I called Eric and told him about Daniel's visit. I was pleased that he didn't overreact. We agreed I would lock the doors and windows and have Harper put his number on speed dial. Then, he said out loud what I had been thinking: "A man who is in his forties doesn't just wake up and decide to assault women. He's been thinking about it for most of his adult life. He may not be successful in acting out his impulses, but now that he has a taste for it, he'll do it again. I'm sure of it. One other thing. Visiting you was an act of fear. You threatened to expose him and all his dirty little secrets. You keep after him and he may crack."

"Good."

•   •   •

I put on a sweater and took a seat on my patio. The LED solar lights illuminated my still dormant plants with a rainbow of soft colors and cast unnatural red and green shadows that danced in a light breeze.

With no energy for introspection, brooding, or self-analysis, I contented myself with listening to the quaking of old leaves that had refused to fall and sipping wine while snuggling in a soft sweater better suited for winter than early spring. I even remained apathetic in the face of an ominous text from Martin:

"The attorney general has called a meeting for tomorrow at eight to review your conduct before Judge Tawney and other matters. Your presence is mandatory. Your favorite bus driver."

A few minutes later, I received a text from Nora Barlow reminding me of a conference call with Francis Akins to discuss the release date of the results of the rape kit backlog project and how she could sort the data to show rape clusters by perpetrator, location, and age of the victim among other groupings. I was about to text Nora to proceed without me when an epiphany jolted me from my indifference. I sat up straight, almost spilling my wine.

Some "aha" moments are accompanied by a serotonin rush and a moment of clarity. This one was shocking and unnerving because, in hindsight, it was obvious: *Daniel Lockhart was a serial rapist.*

Daniel knew the rape kit data would reveal his DNA and expose him for who he was. My objection to the expungement order "hurt" him because he was running out of time. He had to have his DNA data expunged before the rape kit data came online or it would be too late.

I now had a singular goal, something tangible I could accomplish. I would focus all my energy and legal skills to delay the expungement order long enough to get his DNA tested against the rape kit data.

I fumbled with my phone and sent Martin an encrypted text.

"It is imperative to delay the expungement order. Daniel may be a serial rapist. Filing a restraining order against Daniel Lockhart. Will explain tomorrow."

His response was quick and chilling:

"I'm doing what I can, but you have to trust me. At the meeting, don't volunteer anything about Daniel Lockhart, the expungement order, or the jury. If you can avoid speaking tomorrow, all the better. You should brace yourself for questions about whether you endangered Harper by allowing her to attend the demonstration."

I read the text multiple times. How could anyone suspect me of endangering my child?

CHAPTER TWELVE

I slept sporadically, troubled on so many levels by Martin's response. I showered, washed and dried my hair, and put on my best lawyer suit. When Harper sat down, I was already at the kitchen table, reading his message for the umpteenth time.

"Has this town gone crazy, or am I just too young to understand it?"

"Crazy doesn't do it justice," I said without looking up. "You probably understand it better than most."

"Is that bad news?" she asked. "I mean, you look a little pissed off."

I looked up. "Sorry. To answer your question, it's hard to tell. Probably bad, but not sure how. You look so much better."

"You're not the only one." Harper showed me a string of threatening text messages. "I don't know how they got my number. I tried to block them, but they just keep showing up."

The messages were crude, sexist, and worrisome.

"I can ask Eric if he can find out who's sending them."

Harper shook her head. "I'll deal with it. Because you're probably going to be suspended, I was thinking you might have time to make breakfast."

I didn't see the connection but welcomed the distraction. We agreed on French toast and sausage. I ate little, spending my time sipping coffee, gazing at my beautiful daughter, and feeling blessed. The moment lasted until Harper announced she wasn't going to school.

"Well, you are, but not because I'm being a bitch. What I learned last night is that I'm being investigated for child endangerment for letting you go to the demonstration and get tear-gassed. Not showing up today would probably get me arrested and get you a visit from child protection services."

"You didn't endanger me. The stupid governor and his Gestapo did. And I'll just spend most of the morning in the principal's office…"

I raised my hand to cut her off. "Hear me out. I have written a note for you and a statement you can use in case of an emergency. The note reads: 'Please excuse my daughter's absence from class yesterday. I permitted her to attend a demonstration to learn firsthand how precious the rights granted under the First Amendment are and how difficult it is to exercise them. I believe the event was a learning opportunity, and that she benefited greatly from the experience.'"

A broad grin spread across Harper's face. "That's a badass note."

"You may not need it, but if you're asked, present it with steely eyes and determination."

Harper pursed her lips. "And the statement?"

I handed her a piece of paper. "If you're denied admission to your classes, read this statement, then call me and I'll pick you up."

She read it silently, then out loud, her expression morphing slowly from unsure to almost gleeful. "As you know, I have developed a relationship with the media and, in particular, with CNN. You have left me no choice but to redress the denial of my right to attend class publicly and in a court of law."

"Oh my God, I hope they choose to suspend me. That would be pretty awesome to read in front of my friends."

"Save it for when you need it. Try to act like today is any other day. It will give you an aura of mystery."

"Like mother like daughter."

"That," I said. "But if you think anyone is watching you or if you're in the slightest bit fearful, call me or call Eric. I'll text you his number."

"Are you going to be okay?"

"Absolutely. Nothing to worry about."

But there was.

•   •   •

When I arrived at the courthouse, I was determined to take the advice I'd given Harper and act like today was just like any other. The problem was it wasn't.

Martin's assurance he was doing what he could suggested he was engaged in a serious battle over my future. His admonition that I needed to trust him portended an outcome I wouldn't like. That he wanted me to keep quiet about Daniel, the expungement motion, and the jury simply left me wondering.

I was prepared to be disciplined and potentially suspended. Under state law, the attorney general couldn't fire me, but only recommend me to the bar association for disciplinary proceedings. The attorney general could put pressure on Martin to fire me, but I was confident he would slow roll my dismissal. I hadn't had the opportunity to explain why delaying the expungement order was critical, or how I concluded that Daniel Lockhart was a serial rapist, but was confident that Daniel would figure it out. My biggest concern was the specter of being accused of child endangerment.

I was ushered into a conference room where Martin was seated at the head of a large table. He gestured for me to sit next to him without making eye contact. Carl Hinton, the Attorney General, stood at the rear of the room, watching victoriously as Martin prepared to deliver the punishment for my transgressions.

I leaned close to him. "Did you get my message?"

He responded with a stern look and a slight shake of his head. He opened a notebook and cleared his throat before reading a lawyerly text in a formal voice. The gist of the complaint was that I had violated office policy and my ethical obligations as an officer of the court multiple times. These violations included disrespecting a judge, conspiring with defense counsel to obstruct an active prosecution, and intervening in a legal proceeding on behalf of an accused without authorization. This conduct required that I be suspended immediately pending a decision to terminate my employment. Additionally, I was to be referred to the bar association for a disciplinary hearing to determine whether I should remain a member of the bar.

When he finished reading, I smiled at him, then at the attorney general. "Anything else?"

One of the more hackneyed legal rules is never to ask a question unless you know the answer. I was trying to be snarky, but Martin retrieved a document from a folder, sighed, cleared his throat, and then read it to me.

"I must inform you that you are the target of an investigation into whether allowing your daughter, Harper Corbin, to attend a public gathering where the potential for violence was high without adult supervision constituted child endangerment. You will receive a target letter notifying you that if the investigation uncovers evidence of endangerment or neglect, you will face felony charges and Child Protection Services will remove Harper from your custody."

Martin finally made eye contact. His bottom lip was trembling and the corners of his mouth were taut and turned downward. I looked at Carl Hinton. The joy of victory was evident in a broad smile and bright eyes.

I hadn't considered how serious the child endangerment threat was. The formal investigation was the penalty for crossing the governor, the lieutenant governor, the attorney general, and their supporters.

Martin asked for my passkey and the attorney general departed, leaving me alone with my former friend.

I set my jaw and glared at him. "Well, it looks like you mastered the art of throwing someone under the bus."

"Stop," he said wearily.

"You said the moral high ground was a lonely place. Looks like you've made new friends. Hope it works out for you."

He slammed his fist into the table as the word "stop" exploded from his lips. "Can't you get it through your head that we can't save ourselves, much less Sheila Fanning? I'm just trying to buy some time to figure out whether there's any way to draw blood on our way out the door." When I didn't respond, he pushed back from the table, sending his chair against the wall. "You don't have a clue how much fucking trouble you caused me, and what I had to do to keep your ass out of jail."

"I'm sorry… What did you—"

"I had to agree to not run again, or you were going to be arrested on felony contempt of court charges." He grabbed his folder. "Just go home."

He was almost at the door when I said, "Daniel Lockhart is a serial rapist. I think his DNA is in the rape kit data that will be loaded any day now. That's why he was so keen on having his DNA expunged from the database. That's why he came to my house last night and threatened Harper."

Martin spun and faced me. "Wait. Daniel threatened you? What do you mean, serial rapist?" Martin retrieved his chair and returned to the table. "Start over."

"All I have are a few facts connected by a lot of assumptions, but the gist is this. The governor was shopping for a case that would deter doctors from performing abortions under the rape exception. He landed on Sheila's complaint against Daniel. She'd used her claim of rape to get an abortion. I don't know how, but the attorney general knew of the abortion even though we didn't. If Daniel's lawyer could convince the jury that the sex with Sheila was consensual, that she wasn't raped, the rape exception wouldn't apply, and her abortion would be deemed illegal."

"Lots of ifs…"

"I found two jurors that look like ringers."

"What does this have to do with Daniel?"

"Daniel demanded that the attorney general accelerate his trial date. Daniel knew about the rape kit backlog testing project and that his only chance of escaping detection as a serial rapist was to be acquitted and file an expungement motion. The governor thought he was using Daniel, but it was actually the opposite. If we expose Daniel as a serial rapist, he will implicate the governor in jury tampering. So, the expungement order had to be approved."

Martin raised his eyebrows, turned his head, and gave me a sideways glance.

"Are you really saying that the governor knew that Daniel Lockhart was a serial rapist?"

"Maybe not initially, but I think they found out at some point and now have to cover their tracks."

Martin settled back in his chair. "That's some theory."

"Daniel told me he's thinking about representing himself going forward and that he has the ear of the attorney general and the lieutenant governor. The only way Daniel has that kind of access is because he's got some kind of leverage over them. But the proof goes away once his DNA is expunged from the database."

"You're asking me to believe that the governor and his top advisors have conspired to subvert justice and are now trying to cover up their association with a serial rapist by tampering with the State's DNA database?" He shook his head.

"Scoff if it makes you feel better, but what if I'm right? What's the worst that could happen if we assume the governor's office is involved in a conspiracy and a coverup? We embarrass ourselves? Hell. I'm going to be disbarred and labeled an unfit mother. I see little downside in going full red-faced about the governor and Daniel Lockhart."

Martin closed his eyes and emitted a soft groan. "Let's pretend I accept as fact everything you just said. What you don't get is that it doesn't matter. You're living in a world where the truth is determined by unbiased, independent triers of fact. That world is gone. The power to decide what passes as truth rests with Carl Hinton, the governor, and the lieutenant governor. The judge approved the expungement order last night. You can't stop it. Daniel is a free man and will stay that way. If you want to pretend you can fight and win, you'll lose your daughter. I wish it were otherwise."

• • •

I sat in my office bathed in the silence of defeat. I looked at the legal pad in front of me where I intended to outline an approach for proving my allegations against the governor and his attorney general and exposing Daniel Lockhart as a serial rapist. The blank page stared back at me, reflecting what was in my head. I knew the truth, but instead of setting me free, it had given me a monster headache.

Martin had left a guest passkey on my desk, which I could use if other prosecutors need my help to get up to speed on my pending cases. I stared at it, seeing it as the ultimate symbol of surrender. I was no longer officially part of the justice system. More to the point, I felt like a guest in the town I'd grown up in. Governor Adams and his power-hungry associates had successfully imposed their narrow vision of life on Sheila, me, Harper, and the Village of Freeman's Gate. Worse, they controlled the institutions that historically could be used to challenge them. This is what being powerless felt like.

Even more frustrating was how easy it would be to expose Daniel Lockhart as a serial rapist. We could compare his DNA to the rape kit DNA in a few minutes. A positive match would prove he was a serial rapist and force the governor's office to explain what they knew and when they knew it. Simple, straightforward, and determinative.

But laws, rules, and administrative procedures protected the State's DNA database. Even the people who managed the database couldn't access the data without cause. The administrators rigorously maintained access logs. Harsh penalties awaited those who violated the sanctity of the data. If I wanted to expose Daniel Lockhart as a sexual predator, I had to do so in a way that didn't violate the law or his rights.

Even as I fumed and fiddled, I knew the exercise was pointless. With the expungement order approved, Daniel's DNA would be wiped from the state databases and, as long as he wasn't arrested for another crime and a new sample taken, his status as a serial rapist would be unknowable.

I turned my attention to the expungement order that required the state crime lab to delete Daniel's DNA from the state's databases. Like most legal documents, the language seemed repetitive and redundant, largely to prevent lawyers like me from circumventing its intent. I gleaned nothing new from repetitively perusing the words of the first clause, but the language of the second part of the order requesting the deletion of all DNA derived from the person of Sheila Fanning puzzled me. I couldn't understand the point of deleting crime scene data, but I knew someone who might.

I called Nora Barlow's cell phone number.

"Why does a call from you in the early morning make me suspicious?" she said. "Either you're going to tell me you thought of something that will make me hate my job a little less, or I'm going to hang up."

"You are supposed to hate your job, so no. But tell me again about how you process rape evidence. Just the basics."

"Why do I suspect you're trying to find an angle to get me to do something I can't or don't want to do?"

I laughed. "Because you're smart and because I'm transparent. Just humor me."

"The rape kit evidence goes into a database of crime scene data— rape victims are crime scenes—called the forensic database. Of course, we don't know who the DNA belongs to. Another database keeps DNA taken from suspects arrested on suspicion of committing a crime and DNA from those convicted of various crimes. That is the Convicted Offender and Arrestee Index. We take the offender and arrestee data and use it to search the forensic data. If there's a match, we have a suspect who we can investigate and possibly charge. Simple really."

"And the rape kit data will go into the forensic database?"

"When we finish verifying it is in the correct format and not corrupted, yes."

"Hypothetically, if you were to receive an expungement order from an arrestee, it would make sense that he or she would want you to expunge the arrestee's data from the offender and arrestee database.

Why would an arrestee want you to expunge data acquired from a victim from the forensic database?"

"If you're referring to the order about Daniel Lockhart, after deleting Daniel's DNA from the arrestee index, it's as if he was never arrested. Forensic data is another matter. You would only want to delete that data if you thought it could implicate you in other crimes."

"Why do I get the impression you're trying to tell me something?" I asked.

"No, I'm not. We have strict rules about who we can communicate with and about what. You can, however, ask me questions that relate to our work on the rape kit backlog project. Do you have a question, maybe how we analyze forensic data and, more particularly, how we intend to analyze the rape kit data? Take a moment."

"I feel like I'm back in law school," I said.

I had always hated the way law professors answered a question with a question. But Nora had forced me to consider how the data taken from Sheila Fanning could hurt Daniel Lockhart.

"Do you run statistics on the forensic database to determine whether you have multiple victims associated with a single offender?"

"We do and have already looked at groupings in the rape kit data. As I will discuss in our next conference call, we have some clusters suggesting possible multiple rapes by single perpetrators. Next question?"

"When you combine the DNA evidence from the rape kits with the existing forensic data, will you search for clusters again?"

Hearing the question out loud raised the hairs on my arms. "Jesus. Leaving the data taken from Sheila in the database would enable you to determine whether Daniel was the perpetrator represented by one of the clusters in the rape kit data."

I heard Nora chuckle. "That's not a question, so I'm not going to comment either way."

"But I can't imagine either Daniel or his attorney would know this."

Nora sighed. "Probably not, but maybe the attorney general or someone in his office would. For the life of me, I can't imagine why someone in the AG's office would share that with defense counsel. But if you think that's what happened, how do you prove it?"

"Why are we so hung up on having to prove stuff?"

Nora laughed. "That's a little unnerving coming from a prosecutor. Anything else?"

"Daniel can't get away with this. Right? If he's a serial rapist, we can't—"

"You know I can't run a query using Daniel's DNA without a formal request submitted against an active investigation. That was illegal even before the expungement order. Once the order is implemented, it won't matter. The clock on that data is ticking."

"It matters to me. The part that galls me is that the attorney general and his cronies are helping set Daniel free. Why would they do that?"

"Before making that allegation—"

"I know. I have to have sufficient evidence to prove it. Sometimes it seems like it's a lot easier being a bad guy."

"Welcome to my world," said Nora. And with that, she ended the call.

•   •   •

The call with Nora convinced me that my suspicions about Daniel Lockhart were correct and that for reasons I couldn't discern, the attorney general was determined to make sure no one knew about it. I felt vindicated, but the information did nothing to change the stark reality Martin had painted earlier.

I turned my attention to filing a petition for a stalking injunction against Daniel Lockhart. The law defines stalking as "willfully, maliciously, and repeatedly following, harassing, or cyberstalking another person." Fortunately, the process amounted to filing out a form naming the parties involved in the alleged behavior that constituted stalking and filing it with the clerk of the court. If things went my way, the court could issue a temporary injunction immediately, which would be good for a few weeks. If I were really lucky, Daniel would violate the order and the police would arrest and take a new sample of his DNA that wasn't covered by the expungement order.

I printed the form, signed it, and headed to the clerk's office. She read the form and then looked at me.

"He came into your house when your daughter was there alone?"

I nodded.

"I'll see that the judge processes this right away. He's got kids, too. I'm sure we will issue the order today."

Outside the courthouse, I was still enjoying the satisfaction of my victory against Daniel Lockhart when my phone rang. I glanced at the screen, intending to send it to voicemail, when I saw Sheila Fanning's name displayed in large black letters.

"Hi," I said in an animated voice I hoped conveyed a welcoming tone, "how are you?"

For a moment, all I could hear was the sound of rapid breathing and muffled shouting. "Help me," she said, her voice guarded but desperate. "Quinn is—"

She let out a scream, which was immediately followed by a male voice yelling something unintelligible. Another loud noise erupted, and the call ended.

I called Eric. He answered on the first ring. "I know," he said quickly. "We are on our way. Ten minutes tops. I've texted you her address."

I had walked to work and needed to get home to get my car. I ran across the courthouse plaza, wishing I'd worn sneakers instead of my expensive pumps. I was breathless when I got inside the house and surprised to see Harper.

"They canceled class…What's wrong?"

"Quinn attacked Sheila again," I said, grabbing my keys. "I can't talk. I have to go."

"I'm coming with you."

I considered saying no, but her tone suggested it would have been futile.

"You'll stay in the car until I know what's going on. On the way, you can tell me you didn't walk home alone."

•   •   •

It normally would have taken ten minutes to drive to Sheila's apartment complex, but police cars blocked the nearby streets. I parked a few blocks away and wondered whether I'd been better off walking from the courthouse. I texted Eric and told him where I was. Harper made it clear she had no intention of staying in the car, and we hurried back to the police tape, where I spotted Eric talking to a woman who was pointing at the apartment building. The moment he looked at me, I knew Sheila was in trouble. He finished his conversation with the witness, then approached us, his lips pursed, sadness reflected on his face.

"I'm sorry," he said. "We got here too late. We'll take her to the hospital as soon as she's stabilized, but—"

We turned to see a man covered in blood being escorted to a police car. He was shouting obscenities while sobbing. All I could make out was "…the bitch killed my child."

"Is Sheila going to die?" asked Harper.

As the ambulance sped away, the wailing of its siren offered an ominous reply.

CHAPTER THIRTEEN

Harper and I sat in the car, waiting for the police to reopen the streets around the crime scene. She was in no mood to talk and said so. Instead, her focus was on her phone, her thumbs dancing effortlessly as she composed and sent texts into the ether.

I stared at the phone number for Helena Davis while searching for the right words to convey the news about her daughter. When I was convinced there were none, I hit the call button and a moment later heard her voice.

"I know something has happened," said Helena. "I can feel it. Tell me."

"Quinn attacked her, and she hit her head. I wish I could tell you she'll be all right. I think you should get here as soon as possible."

"Thank you. I…"

I could hear her breathing, short shallow breaths of someone looking over the edge of panic but resisting stoically.

"Last night I had a dream about her," she said. "Sheila was asking me about her favorite dress and if I could bring it to her. I don't have it anymore. So much is lost…"

"I'm so sorry, Helena." My words sounded hollow and cliched, probably because they were.

The call ended. I resisted the urge to scream.

"Can we go home now?" asked Harper.

We said nothing more.

At home, Harper retreated to the sanctuary of her room. I craved the company of a glass of wine on my patio, but the ringing of my phone thwarted my plan. The number that appeared on the screen was unknown to me, and the caller's name wasn't displayed. Normally, I would ignore such calls, but I was unsure whether it was news about Sheila. I pressed "answer," greeted the caller with a cold "yes," and waited with my thumb on the "end call" button.

"This is Dr. Palmer. I performed the abortion for Sheila Fanning."

"I know who you are," I said. "What can I do for you?"

"One of my nurses told me what happened to her and that she's in the ICU with severe head injuries. I wanted to call because…I don't know. If you don't know already, the attorney general's office offered me a deal, and I took it."

"A deal?" A moment later, the meaning became clear. "He dropped the charges against you. Of course you took the deal."

"But…I'm sorry. I thought I could make myself feel better, but I can't. I shouldn't have called."

"Wait," I said. "You might earn a little solace if you tell me how the attorney general knew Sheila had an abortion?"

"I wish I could. As part of my deal, I'm not allowed to discuss the case with anyone other than my lawyer."

I heard a loud sigh, followed by a softer one. Dr. Palmer was wavering, apparently trying to referee a battle between her conscience and what her lawyer instructed her to do. "You think I'm a coward, and maybe I am. But I'm also a realist. I've invested over twenty years of my life in building my practice. I live well, some might say, beyond my means. I like country clubs and travel and have kids in Ivy League colleges. I know power when I see it. The governor and his administrators have it. You don't. I have enough to get my way at the club, but I don't have near enough to keep from being prosecuted."

"Are you trying to make a point?"

"You should see this situation practically and not as a challenge to your values. They matter little when everything you cherish is taken from you. Think of your daughter and let this go."

"I am thinking of her. Tell me who knew about Sheila's abortion and how they found out."

Dr. Palmer didn't answer, but she didn't hang up. After a brief silence, she cleared her throat. "A group paid one of my administrators to report the names of patients. After abortion became illegal, the reward for reporting an actual abortion was quite high. I suspected something, but you know, I just let it pass. I think they were also tracking patients through their phones. That's all I know."

"What was the name of the group?"

I waited a moment for an answer that never came, then tossed my phone on the kitchen counter.

I turned on the TV and poured a glass of wine. CNN was covering Sheila's beating as "breaking news." At first, the reporters were circumspect when it came to discussing what provoked her husband, Quinn, to attack her, alluding only to social media reports that the child she aborted was his and not Daniel Lockhart's, the man she accused of raping her. One reporter was adamant there was no evidence whose child it was, but regardless, Sheila's husband believed the unsubstantiated posts. The story, they said, was still evolving and would be updated. The network couldn't—or wouldn't—lay the blame where it belonged, closing with a cryptic, "We are awaiting the reactions of Governor Warren Adams and Lieutenant Governor Tanya Cobb."

I left the talking heads to rehash the facts among themselves and knocked on Harper's door. A voice told me to leave her alone, that she didn't want to talk, and that there was nothing for me to say.

At least I had tried. I returned for my glass of wine and took refuge on the patio. The air was warm and insects buzzed energetically. Overnight, or so it seemed, buds appeared on the azaleas, and tulips and daffodils were in full bloom. Change was everywhere, and I reveled in it.

Harper plopped in the chair next to me just as my phone buzzed for the umpteenth time. I looked at the screen, saw the word "MOM" at the top, and hit voicemail.

"Who was that?"

"My mother. Nothing important."

"Have you heard anything about Sheila?"

My phone buzzed again. "It's just my mother," I said, anticipating a question. "Nothing yet. How are you?"

"Miserable, I guess. I don't know. Do you think we should move somewhere else? I don't like it here anymore."

I patted her hand. "The thought has occurred to me, but where would we go? I'm done being a prosecutor. I thought I could make a difference. Maybe we both need a fresh start, but we shouldn't do anything impulsive. Maybe I could get a job at a plant nursery." A moment of silence was followed by laughter. "Just thinking out loud."

The third time my phone buzzed, Harper said, "Take it. She'll just keep trying."

I hesitated, then pressed "answer."

"Hi, Mom. This isn't a good time."

"It's never a good time to talk to me," she said matter-of-factly, "but I saw you on TV with the governor and Tanya Cobb. I wanted you to know how proud I am that you're supporting their efforts to protect the unborn."

I puffed my cheeks and groaned softly. "Why do you do this, Mom? I'm not going to have this argument with you again. Not now. Not ever."

"Your dad..."

"I don't care. I'm going to hang up. Don't call again."

I looked at Harper. "I'm sorry you heard that."

She looked away. "You don't talk about it, but I think it has something to do with me. It makes me sad when I think it's my fault."

"No, sweetie. You can't think like that. It's complicated and there's no point...Some stories are best not told."

Harper turned and stared at me unblinking, her jaw set. "But it's my story, too."

I drained my glass of wine. "The other day, you said you weren't interested in knowing the details of what happened to me. This won't be easy for me to tell or you to hear. Nod if you agree to listen before you decide to hate me like I hate my mother."

She nodded, but the scowl on her face suggested she was leaving her options open.

"My parents raised three kids. My older brothers were always getting into trouble and were always forgiven. I was getting good grades in school, but because I was a girl, neither seemed to care. That is, unless I screwed up. Typical double standard kind of stuff."

"You never talk about your brothers."

"Trust me, you wouldn't like them. I couldn't wait to get away from them and my parents. When I left for college, I was determined to do what I wanted, to have fun without being judged. Of course, I thought I was smart enough to have fun and stay out of trouble. I wasn't. No one told me about drinking and date-rape drugs. At a frat party, a guy handed me a cup of what I thought was punch. Whatever it was, it was laced with something, and I was sexually assaulted. I don't remember the event clearly and couldn't say with certainty who assaulted me. Before I had recovered from the rape, I realized I was pregnant. I tried to pretend I wasn't, but eventually, I had to tell my parents."

Tears streamed down Harper's cheeks. She started to leave, but I grabbed her arm. "I only have the strength to tell this story once. Just let me finish."

She folded her arms across her chest. "Whatever."

"My parents were right-to-lifers. When I broke the news, Mom grabbed her Bible. Dad lost his mind. He wondered how he could face his friends at the country club. How could I ruin their lives? How could I make the mistake only bad girls made? They never asked me how I was coping. It was about them. Always about them. Dad said getting pregnant was my sin, and I had to take care of it."

"Meaning what?"

I shrugged. "They were anti-abortion but sending me code that I should sin again and have one. I was left to decide on my own. At nineteen, I had to decide to go against everything I grew up believing about the sanctity of life. But I also had to deal with the dreams I had for my future. I was going to study law and maybe practice international law in the Hague. Thoughts of travel and adventure filled my head. No way was I ready to be a mother. I had a decision to make and time was running out. With no one to talk to, I thought about killing myself."

Harper was sobbing, her body shaking. "Please stop. I don't want to hear anymore."

I wiped tears from my eyes. "I'm almost done. I was on my way to an abortion clinic for the third time, still conflicted when fate stepped in. A truck ran a red light and crushed my car, leaving me in a coma. The accident left me badly hurt, but you were fine. By the time I recovered from my injuries and a stubborn infection, it was too late for an abortion. My parents had arranged for an adoption, but I refused. I always wanted you and have loved you from the day you were born."

"Enough…"

"When Mom and Dad came into my hospital room, you were in my arms. I can't describe how happy I was at that moment. I showed you to them, expecting that seeing you would bring them joy, but my mother wouldn't look at you. Then she said, 'If you keep that child, don't come home.' That's your story. That's how you ended up with me, and I became an orphan of sorts. All I can hope for now is that you don't hate me."

She bolted from her chair and into the house. My secret had found its way into the open. I slid away from the table, fighting back the sadness rising from the depth of my being. I made it to my bedroom before tremors wracked my body. I let them in and indulged them. I knew this day would come. I knew it would hurt, although not how much.

•   •   •

Later that evening, I returned to the kitchen and cleared the dishes from lunch. Harper appeared, her eyes puffy and red, and sat down.

"I don't hate you," she said. "I've always felt different. Everyone knows my mom wasn't married. I just don't know why life is so complicated."

"Humans are complicated animals," I said, "and flawed. I am living proof." I took her hands and continued. "Understand that there is a difference between having a choice, which all women should have, and the choice you make. Choices are made for reasons that shouldn't have to be explained. But don't think it's easy. If you're going to choose to have a child, you can't resent the child for the price you have to pay. If you decide not to have a child, you can't feel sorry for yourself if it saddles you with guilt. I didn't choose to have you, but I chose to keep you, love you, and treat you with respect. If my life isn't what I planned, I don't care. That's the truth, no matter what my parents think."

"Thank you for keeping me," she said with a soft laugh. "I can be challenging."

"I wouldn't want you any other way. If I wanted non-challenging, I would have adopted a hamster."

Harper fixed her gaze on me. "How do you do that? Sheila is in the hospital. You may be fired, and it seems everyone is mad at you. Mr. Lockhart is going to get away with raping Sheila, and yet you just blow it off."

"Don't kid yourself, sweetie. Your mother can be a raging cat when cornered. But being pissed won't solve anything. Being smart might. I'm trying to be smart, but it's not going so well at the moment."

"Tell me you will make Mr. Lockhart go to jail."

"I'm working on it. The judge approved the restraining order I filed. So that's something."

"And Tanya Cobb? I can't stand her."

"Probably not, although I think she'd look good in an orange jumpsuit. We'll see."

My phone signaled the arrival of a new text from Eric Graham. Just when it seemed life had dished out enough misery, there was more.

Sheila Fanning was dead.

CHAPTER FOURTEEN

The news of Sheila's death made Harper inconsolable. I quickly ran out of words and let her cry herself numb.

After she recovered, we had a brief chat about what was going to happen now that she was dead. The police would investigate her husband, Quinn, and charge him with second-degree murder. The best he might do is accept a plea of involuntary manslaughter. Either way, he was going to prison for a long time. The answer wasn't satisfying.

"What about Daniel and Tanya and the people that sent him messages and texts about Sheila cheating on him? Shouldn't they go to jail?"

Rather than get into the weeds of the law of incitement, I opted for a simple yes and asked if she wanted to join Eric and me at the Shade Tree Café. She declined but promised me she was all right.

When I arrived, Eric had already taken a seat. He announced he'd ordered two cappuccinos and would drink mine if I didn't want it. He looked at me and then closed his eyes. "I'm sorry. I'll admit to being cranky if you agree not to take it personally."

"That works for me."

The facts were just coming in, but her husband, Quinn, was receiving texts from an anonymous source that included photos of Sheila with other men in compromising positions. Sheila insisted they were fake, but they made Quinn furious. He started drinking and then picked a fight with her. The neighbors said it was nasty and called us right away. Before the police could respond, he'd hit her. She fought back, but then she hit her head on the edge of a stone countertop in the bathroom. She was brain-dead before she hit the floor.

I gritted my teeth. "This is Daniel's doing. He drove Quinn to kill Sheila. I want Daniel to suffer. I want him to pay."

"Don't do anything stupid. The last thing I want to do is arrest you."

"Define stupid."

Eric laughed. "One could argue about where the line is these days. Don't shoot him where there are video cameras or with a gun that is registered to you. Make sure you don't load a gun with bullets without wearing gloves. Actually, it's a long list, and this isn't the time or place to go through it. Maybe later?"

"I could charge him with incitement. Maybe I could charge Tanya Cobb while I'm still in a good mood."

Eric shook his head. "You know that's a waste of time. It's hard to prove and the attorney general won't support it."

"Not to mention that the attorney general made Martin suspend me and investigate me for child endangerment."

"Anyone who knows you knows you wouldn't endanger Harper. That's just nuts."

The cappuccinos arrived. I dipped a spoon into the whipped cream and was underwhelmed, making me wonder if decadence was best enjoyed when in a good mood. I took a few sips and then sat back.

"What have you heard about the governor's office spying on patients at women's health clinics?"

Eric shrugged. "Not much. I hear stories about geofence warrants, but technology-based warrants require expertise most cops don't have. I know someone who may know the IT guy in the governor's office. If he's smart, he won't talk to you. Some of those guys don't like government snooping, even as they snoop for a living. But I don't see what it would accomplish. The governor's cult controls the agencies that would investigate his office for corruption. It's hard to imagine they would fire one of their own."

"The bad guys win?"

"It's their ball, their game, and they write the rules. We elected them, so we can only blame ourselves."

I drank the rest of the cappuccino and then sloshed the whipped cream that had settled at the bottom of the cup. "My former boss lost his career because of me. My best friend is an aging cop who likes expensive coffee that I'm not sure I can afford anymore. My daughter knows more about her mother's past than I'd like. And this will come as a surprise, but I'm a terrible loser. I'm thinking of keying the governor's car and throwing a pie in the face of his fat, arrogant lieutenant. Something about the grin on Daniel's face is like a bruise I can't stop pressing. I'm thinking bad thoughts. Worse, I'm whining about it."

"You want me to plant drugs in his car or tell some guys on the street he's a snitch?"

"Would you? Probably not a good idea. I want him exposed for what he is. I'm just not sure how to do it legally."

Eric moved closer. "You need to be careful. This morning, I looked at Daniel's file on the departmental computer. I knew right away someone had deleted portions of the original file. But the detective who is handling his case is an old-school guy who likes paper more than computers and has a hard copy of the original. He let me look at a psych evaluation that was ordered when Daniel was first incarcerated. Apparently, Daniel was having problems adjusting to being locked up and was on suicide watch."

"Might have been better not to watch him."

"Point taken. To continue, Daniel isn't just sociopathic but is fearful of being controlled by people smarter than him, particularly women. The conclusion is he is more likely a danger to others than himself, especially if cornered. But someone deleted all that from his official file, which explains why you didn't see it, and neither did his arraignment judge. We lock up a guy charged with petty theft, but we let a socio-psychiatric time bomb out on bail? Makes sense in someone's world. Just not mine."

I shrugged. "Makes you wonder if an invisible hand isn't guiding things."

"Daniel may be sick and possibly dangerous, but the bail judge saw him as a first offender. After the trial, he's just a guy who had sex with a married woman who felt bad about it afterward. Adultery is like jaywalking. Even good people do it, so it's not a crime anymore."

I laughed. "I think it used to be. These days, the man gets a high-five from his friends for screwing his best friend's wife. The married woman earns the reputation of being loose and immoral. Nothing ever changes."

Eric studied me for a moment. "Let me put it this way. Daniel isn't someone you should mess with. He's a danger to you and Harper. A restraining order won't stop him. You might want to consider leaving him be."

"That would be the sensible thing to do," I said, nodding. "The attorney general intervened, and the judge granted his expungement order, despite my objections. Daniel's DNA has been purged from the state databases or will be soon. He's a serial rapist, and he's going to go free. There's nothing left for me to do. All of that is a hard pill to swallow."

Eric left, but I wasn't ready to leave. Maybe it was the caffeine or the chocolate, but I couldn't shake the feeling I had said something or read something important. For a few minutes, I searched aimlessly on the internet, clicking on news stories but reading only the first few lines. Whatever it was, I couldn't retrieve the thought. I gave up and headed home.

•　　•　　•

When I walked into the kitchen, Harper was drinking a soda. She looked at me, her puffy eyes making it clear she'd been watching news coverage about Sheila. I turned down the volume of the TV and sat next to her at the kitchen table. She avoided looking at me, her attention focused instead on her drink.

The events in the Village of Freeman's Gate had taken over the news cycle for the last several days. Sheila's death was another breaking news opportunity to rehash her rape trial, her arrest, the riots, and even Harper's interview and T-shirt. Most segments included speculation about the governor's plans to run for president and how Sheila's arrest factored into his chances nationally. With her death, the perspective had changed to how the governor's pursuit of a woman who many believed had been raped might hurt his political future.

Of course, the talking heads didn't know about the corrupted jury, the government's spying campaign, or how Tanya's "soldiers" had incited Sheila's husband into becoming a wife killer. They certainly had no clue that I suspected Daniel Lockhart, the sad victim of a woke-inspired prosecution and the new best friend of Tanya Cobb, of being a serial rapist.

Sheila Fanning's story, depending on whether an investigative reporter discovered new information, could live for days or it could also be pushed off the front page by a more compelling disaster. But for now, it was great for ratings and the media would rehash it nonstop.

Harper finished her drink, announced she couldn't watch anymore of "that shit," and stomped off. I felt the impulse to comment on her word choice, but it was short-lived. The word "shit" was perfect and no socially acceptable substitute would convey the sentiment nearly as well.

I heard Sheila's name, and it drew me back to the TV. Her face was projected next to the text announcing breaking news. A young woman stared into a camera, her expression both earnest and somber:

"Sheila Fanning, the woman arrested just two days ago for an illegal abortion, is dead. She was apparently killed by her husband in a domestic dispute. The story is still developing, but the Lieutenant Governor, Tanya Cobb, initially posted a message that seemed to celebrate the young woman's demise."

A text box flashed on the screen:

"God works through His agents to punish the wicked. God chose Sheila's husband for this important work and we pray for his soul."

The young journalist continued her reporting:

"That message was soon deleted and we haven't been able to reach the lieutenant governor for comment. Sheila Fanning had accused this man, Daniel Lockhart, of rape. When he was acquitted, she was charged with having an illegal abortion. The charges against her spawned demonstrations and drew criticism from women here and abroad."

A picture of Daniel Lockhart flashed on the screen. As galling as Tanya's words were, it was the smirk on Daniel's face, a man who had beaten a rape charge and threatened me and my daughter, that quickened my breathing and clenched my teeth. Asked to comment on Sheila's death, he was indifferent. The woman he'd sexually assaulted had just died and all he could muster was:

"I didn't know her very well. I mean, I didn't rape her, and I didn't kill her. I mean, sometimes, shit happens. It did to me."

The anchor was revisiting the history of the trial, but my thoughts turned to the face of a young woman who, in her own words, "was just doing my job," when Daniel Lockhart forced himself on her. While the media would eventually lose interest in her, Sheila would always be a part of my life. In that moment, I realized that I, too, had been chosen—not by God but by my conscience—to make certain Daniel didn't harm anyone else. All I needed was a little divine inspiration as to how to accomplish the task.

●   ●   ●

Harper and I spent Thursday evening in a silence that was both civil and non-offensive. We both needed space and time to process the emotional wounds inflicted by the events of the last few days. We were talked out.

With Harper in bed, I took a hot bath, changed into my pajamas, and padded around the kitchen. I was mentally numb and hoping to keep it that way. Despite my intentions, I turned on the television but pretended not to watch or listen. That attempt at self-deception failed as the screen displayed the excerpts of the latest social media posts about Sheila. The voice of the female anchor tasked with reporting these posts grew louder, her strident tone revealing a wave of personal anger. She had lost the ability to remain objective and, in doing so, acquired a degree of humanity that made her more likable. She had also revived my simmering anger.

I would have thought Sheila's death would have sobered Tanya's followers, but from their posts, it was clear Sheila wasn't the beneficiary of their loving thoughts and prayers. A common theme was she had killed her baby and deserved to die. A few who saw the bigger picture realized that her death meant that the rape exception remained untested in court.

With nothing left to clean and no reason to keep listening to the news, I turned off the television and collapsed on my bed, exhausted and discouraged.

Sheila deserved better.

CHAPTER FIFTEEN

I was up early the next morning. Breakfast was a reheated cup of coffee and two ibuprofen. I turned on the television, pushed by a faint hope that someone had discovered the truth about Daniel Lockhart and shot him overnight. But the news cycle had to be filled with fresh tragedies. A shooting at a school pep rally in Texas had overtaken Sheila's saga. I watched for a few minutes until a spokesperson for the governor of that state said it was time to arm students and teachers. The talking heads all started yammering at once and the discussion became more about sound bites than an exchange of ideas. I exercised my power over stupidity by turning the TV off and drinking my stale coffee in silence.

Harper strolled into the kitchen and poured a glass of juice before suggesting it would be better if she didn't go to school. I simply said that wasn't a good idea, and she departed. Her lack of protest confirmed what I suspected—even she yearned for life to return to something akin to normal.

But normal wasn't on my agenda. In fact, I couldn't imagine a normal quite like the one I'd lived before Daniel Lockhart had intruded into my world. I hadn't figured out a way around the DNA database procedures, but I had an idea of how I could bait the attorney general into revealing what he knew about Daniel's history. All I needed was Nora Barlow's help. Again.

She answered immediately, and offered a preemptive, "No," revealing an attitude that was predisposed to decline whatever favor I might request.

"That's harsh."

"I know Sheila's dead, and I know you want to make someone pay, but no matter how compelling your argument, it's not going to be me or my staff."

"What if no one has to pay? What if I just want to see what cards the attorney general is holding?"

"I'm sure you won't like this, but I'll give you two minutes to say what's on your mind and then I'm going to say 'no' and hang up."

"First, you call a meeting of the rape kit task force and report that you have fully complied with an expungement order and deleted Daniel Lockhart's DNA records from the arrestee database. You neglect to say you deleted Sheila's data from the forensic database."

"You're aware I've done both?"

"Just listen. With that out of the way, you announce that sorting the rape kit data revealed several potential serial rapists."

"I've done that already, and it did. I haven't reported it yet, but it's on my list."

"Good to know. But you also report that you can't go live with the rape kit data because of a possible anomaly in the forensic database."

"An anomaly? That sounds bad."

"Nothing dramatic. You report that when the rape kit data was added to the existing forensics database, the count of one of the suspected serial rapists increased by one, meaning either the database is corrupted or the serial killer identified in the rape kit data is also in the existing forensic database. Characterize the issue as minor and state you are working to identify the cause of the anomaly if there is one or, if possible, the contributor of the additional data point."

"Let me get this straight. You want Francis Akins to believe that Daniel Lockhart can be identified as a serial rapist from the forensic database? Why would you want her to believe that?"

"Because she will tell the attorney general and if the attorney general knows Daniel is a serial rapist, he will ask you to confirm that you've expunged Sheila Fanning's evidence. At that point, you can confirm that it was, that you did your job, and the error was just a repetitive entry that has since been deleted."

I heard a series of snorts and what sounded like a chuckle. "You are a devious one. It doesn't prove anything but—"

"Can you do that and not get anyone fired?"

"I'll get back to you."

"I'll send you an invitation to Blind Eye. It's an encrypted app used by criminals to keep communications private."

"For the love of God! When you're afraid of your own government, what's the point of having one?"

I left the question unanswered.

"Fine. Just send it."

Nora was correct that even if the attorney general reacted to the ruse and revealed knowledge of Daniel's past crimes, without Daniel's DNA, I couldn't prove he'd raped anyone. But I needed to know who knew what before I could devise a plan to expose the lot of them. If I could trap Daniel, I might persuade him to rat on his protectors.

I made fresh coffee and then opened a folder on my laptop where I kept my notes and records about Sheila's case. Part of me hoped to find something I missed, something I might use against Daniel, while another part of me worried that the something I missed may have saved Sheila.

I pointed the cursor at the first file and clicked it open. Two cups of coffee and a sweet roll later, finding nothing useful, I ended my postmortem. Aside from asking a few more questions to my expert witness, I would handle the case today exactly as I did last week. I was debating what to do next when I received a call from Liz.

"Helena arrived late last night and wants someone to accompany her to the morgue to identify her daughter's body. I can't. I just…"

"Drive her to the hospital. I'll meet you there."

"Thank you. I'm…thank you."

I was in the hospital lobby when they arrived. I took Helena's hand, but she pulled it back.

"The morgue is on the lower level," I said, doing my best to hide my embarrassment. "A police officer and a hospital attendant are waiting, but I must warn you that Sheila suffered severe head wounds that the doctors treated, but they haven't been addressed by a mortician. There was a lot of bruising and swelling and…"

"I've seen dead bodies before. Just show me where I'm supposed to go, and I'll deal with it."

A police officer directed us to a small room containing a gurney covered by a white sheet. My experience with dead people is limited to viewings at funerals. On each occasion, a skilled undertaker had processed the deceased to look peaceful, as if sleeping. When the sheet was pulled back from Sheila's head, it took all my strength to remain vertical. The once beautiful woman was gone, her lovely, childlike face covered with dark purple and yellow bruises and frozen in an expression of pain and disbelief.

Helena stared motionless, only a quick sigh hinting at the shock she felt from seeing her daughter's mutilated face. With a nod, the orderly pulled the sheet over Sheila's remains and the moment ended. A police officer waited for us outside the room where Helena confirmed the deceased was her daughter, Sheila, and signed a paper attesting to the fact.

Back in the lobby, I asked if there was anything I could do.

"Help me, or help you? I know you feel responsible, but you shouldn't. And no. There's nothing you can do to help me. I have lost the person I loved most in this world, and for what? To advance someone's political agenda? I'm still grieving for her father after all these years. I don't have a lot of grief left in me. What I have is anger and rage and it's looking for a place to land. I have lots of thoughts…"

"This is where I'm supposed to tell you not to do anything stupid."

Helena gave me a defiant look. "No one was held accountable when her father was killed. The police department's lawyer offered me money, money I needed to care for myself and my daughter. I had to choose between a slight chance for justice and security. I chose the latter and have lived with that decision for years. If you want to help me, you will find out who's responsible for ending her life and use the law to punish them. If you don't, or can't, I will, no matter how long it takes. Now, I need to see where my daughter died."

•   •   •

I called Eric and arranged for Helena to gain entry to Sheila's townhouse. Technically, the townhouse was still a crime scene, but the investigators had already gathered whatever evidence they needed to confirm Quinn killed her.

Despite Helena's protests, her visit was conditioned on having Eric present. My presence wasn't necessary, but Eric said he'd feel more comfortable if I joined them.

Sheila and Quinn lived in River Walk, a development of townhomes that at one time offered good value for couples just starting out. But a lack of maintenance and years of neglect had relegated River Walk to a venue of last resort. People lived here because they had to and for no other reason. With Quinn unemployed and Sheila working her way through law school, River Walk was all they could afford.

Eric lifted the crime tape and opened the front door. The three of us stepped into a small foyer. To the right was a living room. To the left was a dining room. Pieces of shattered plates littered the floors of both. A jumble of overturned chairs and paintings ripped from the walls made navigating the small rooms challenging. A hole had been punched in the drywall between a metal cross and a portrait of Jesus. Even more disturbing was a dark red handprint captured by a white cloth that still adorned a walnut dining room table. What had once been a home was now a battlefield that exuded rage and its aftershocks.

The neighbors on either side must have heard the commotion and wondered whether the fight was like the ones that preceded it. But sadly, this clash would be the last confrontation. One participant would soon be dead, and the other incarcerated. Neither was coming back.

Eric cautioned Helena not to look in the bathroom, but she was undeterred. Upon seeing the blood splatter on the fixtures, floor, and wall, her only comment was a soft groan.

Our last stop was a small bedroom on the second floor, left untouched by the battle that had consumed the lower level.

"This was Sheila's room," said Helena.

She walked around, touching an assortment of pictures, stuffed animals, and mementos her daughter had collected and cherished. "She didn't sleep with him because she didn't have the money for birth control pills, and she didn't want to get pregnant. Quinn would drink too much and then come on to her. That's what they fought about before the trial. Afterward, it was about whose baby she aborted, but it couldn't have been Quinn's." She squeezed a stuffed bear. "She loved him, or what he was before his world crashed around him. He was ultimately a weak man, and it cost Sheila her life."

She wrapped her arms around the stuffed animal, held it for a moment, then tossed it on the bed. "I'd like to take the things in this room home with me."

Eric explained it wasn't possible but promised to pack Sheila's things and bring them to her when the investigation was officially closed.

Helena sat on Sheila's bed, then put her head on her daughter's pillow and closed her eyes. We left her to mourn on her own. A few minutes later, she declined a ride to her car and left us without a word.

After seeing the crime scene, I also walked home.

• • •

Sheila's death was an embarrassment for the Village of Freeman's Gate. One media critic described the town as "a small place for small-minded people with lots of hateful attitudes." It was, however, a victory of sorts for the governor. In a national poll, respondents viewed his willingness to bring criminal charges against a woman and her doctor who used the rape exception in the abortion law as a pretext to circumvent the abortion ban as a positive attribute and one that proved he was objective about enforcing the law. That the state had dropped the charges against the doctor, and Sheila had died, didn't seem to factor into the responders' thinking.

Curiously, I was also a beneficiary of Sheila's death. A few days after she died, I received an email from Martin advising me I had been returned to full-time status and was no longer a target of an investigation into child endangerment. That was the good news. The bad news was that I was still subject to investigation by the bar association and, because he decided not to run for another term as State Attorney, it was likely his successor would replace all the lawyers in the office who weren't acceptable to the attorney general. We both knew I was at the top of that list and, by fall, would be unemployed.

A new start. The thought pleased me. I imagined where I might live, near the ocean perhaps, or in the mountains. Even better, I'd let Harper choose. But as satisfying as these thoughts were, I was left with the empty feeling that I'd be running away, leaving Daniel and the governor's political machine unchallenged. A new start sounded more and more like an act of cowardice, and the momentary joy evaporated.

CHAPTER SIXTEEN

Harper, too, needed a change of scenery. When she returned from school, she announced that one of her classmates had invited her to a sleepover. She wasn't asking permission but stating a conclusion. I found her surly but was too tired to care. An evening alone sounded like a gift.

Being alone when you're happy is one thing. An evening to reflect on identifying a body and visiting a bloody crime scene was something else. I tried to distract myself by watching old movies without success. The rom-coms were too stupid to amuse me and the thrillers offered so much gratuitous violence I decided I hated the good guys and the bad guys equally.

With Harper gone and the TV off, the house was eerily quiet. The setting was perfect for drinking alone and feeling sorry for myself, but even that option failed to excite me. Instead, I curled up on the sofa with a photo album that featured me and Harper. I lingered over her baby pictures and the days she learned to walk and ride a bike, my heart swelling with each smiling, giggling image of my precious girl.

I fell asleep on the couch clutching the album and feeling blessed.

·   ·   ·

I awoke Saturday morning to clouds and rain and it suited me. Gathering coffee and my phone, I retreated to the patio where the soothing sound of raindrops dancing off leaves serenaded me. The ambiance was blissfully relaxing, at least until my thoughts turned to Harper. She hadn't called, which caused me to vacillate between being relieved and being worried. I was navigating this dilemma when the number for Rose Compton popped up on my screen.

"I can't believe she's dead," she said. "I heard her husband was reading a lot of crap about her cheating on him. That true?"

The question brought a loud sigh, partly because it was sad and partly because I didn't want to think or talk about it.

"It is," I said.

"Some of the jury members have been chatting about what we done and how this is our fault."

"It isn't. You can't blame…" I heard the front door open. "Just a minute."

Harper plopped into a chair next to me. "Who are you talking to? Is it about arresting Daniel Lockhart?"

I shook my head.

"You there? Even one juror who pressed for Daniel's acquittal got a good case of the guilts and rightfully so," said Rose. "She'd like to call you, but only if you agree not to record it or get her in trouble. Can she do that?"

"The case is closed. No one's going to get into trouble, although I don't see the point in revisiting a verdict that can't be changed."

"She's got something to get off her chest, you know. If you'll talk to her, she'll stop bothering me. Her name is Denise Banks. I'll tell her. I gotta feed Sparky and give him his medicine."

"Give Sparky my regards," I said, and the call ended.

"Who's Sparky?"

"A Siamese cat. Handsome and lovable but spoiled. You'd like him. Anyway, that was the forewoman of the jury that acquitted Daniel Lockhart. They're feeling guilty about not convicting him, and I'm the one they think can make them feel better. I can't and even if I could, I don't have it in me today. How was last night?"

"Fine. I guess. We talked about Sheila and watched some of *The Handmaid's Tale*. It was too gross, so we turned it off."

My phone buzzed and played a tone indicating an unknown caller.

"Damn it. One second. This is Ashley Corbin."

"Rose said I could call you. I have something to say, but I'll deny it if you tell anyone. I'm going to say my piece, but I won't answer any questions."

"I'm listening.

"I'm calling from a payphone at the drugstore. I'm a friend of Tanya Cobb and a member of her Soldiers of the Savior—that's her anti-abortion group focused on protecting the unborn and punishing sinners. That may sound made up, but it's the group's value proposition. The group includes Lieutenant Governor Tanya Cobb, Judge Tawney's wife Felicity, and Attorney General Carl Hinton. We use fertility apps, pregnancy help services, geofence warrants, and a tip line to get information about women seeking abortions. The tip line is mostly used by someone in a clinic's admissions office to report the name of a patient and what the visit was for. We pay the snitch in cash, but I don't know how much. After *Roe* was overruled, we also used geofence warrants to track people who frequented the clinics. We recently started collecting data about women who had miscarriages."

"What has any of this to do with Sheila Fanning?"

"Who is that?" asked Harper.

I leaned close to her and angled the phone toward her ear. "A juror," I said softly. "Just listen."

"If you'll shut up, I'll tell you."

"Sorry."

"When the old abortion law went into effect, Tanya became obsessed with making sure the exceptions for rape, incest and protecting the mother's life weren't being used to get around the abortion ban. More recently, she focused the group's efforts on the rape exception. Carl used his office to get geofence warrants and to create a database that correlated rape complaints and abortions. Tanya used the phone numbers to get warrants for phone records. My job was to take the geofence warrant results and the snitch reports, put a name to a visit, and highlight any info about respected citizens, meaning campaign donors and supporters, who were accidentally caught in the net. The AG used that data to edit the list."

"Give me an example of someone whose name he struck from your list."

"Like Phoebe Adams, the only child of Governor Adams."

Harper looked at me and mouthed the words, "Oh my God."

"So connected people get a pass, but everyone else goes on your shit list?"

"Spoken like a liberal with an attitude. I'm trying to do you a favor…"

"Sorry. Sometimes my attitude gets provoked. Please continue."

The phone went silent and for a moment, I thought I'd lost her.

"I believed in the group's objectives and still do, but I didn't know what they were going to put Sheila through. Now it feels dirty spying on those women. Earlier today, Tanya texted me that God had used Sheila's husband as an instrument of punishment for her sins and that she would live in purgatory for eternity. I didn't sign up for getting someone killed. I can't sleep—"

"I'm sorry to interrupt you, but none of this matters now. I appreciate you coming forward, but the case against Sheila has been closed and there is no active investigation."

"You're not listening. There is. My job was to create a list of abortions that were performed based on the rape exception. Those women are going to be prosecuted. I've put that list and some other stuff in an envelope and will leave it in the phone book at the drugstore. Don't contact me. I won't answer questions or testify."

"Just one…Who told you to lie to get on the jury?"

I heard breathing, and the caller cleared her throat. "Tanya. She told me how to say the right things to make sure I wasn't struck. Goodbye."

With the call ended, Harper and I stared at each other.

"Was that for real?" she asked.

"It sounded like it. We'll know when I get back from the drugstore."

"How about I come with you and we get donuts from the bakery?"

I pointed out that I could just pick them up, and she smirked. "You try to get the healthy ones. I like to pick my own."

I considered questioning the concept of a healthy donut, but let it pass.

•   •   •

The rain had stopped, and we chose to walk. Harper was curious about various aspects of the conversation with the juror. I tried to explain why the juror, possibly an older person, might opt to leave an actual document in the drugstore when she could have sent it in a text. Next, Harper asked me to explain why anyone would pay to use a phone, much less the reason behind printing books of phone numbers.

The most troubling and intellectually interesting topic was geofence warrants.

"You're saying it's okay for the government to search a database to find out if my phone has been near a certain location? That's not right. That's Big Brother stuff."

"Other than realizing my daughter has read a banned book, I agree it feels like being spied upon. Sometimes, like a kidnapping of a child or murder, for example, there could be probable cause to get a warrant to track phone location data. But Tanya Cobb and her friends have been using these warrants to identify whole groups of people who frequent abortion clinics without meeting the probable cause threshold. And yes, that's Big Brother stuff for sure."

The drugstore was a ten-minute walk from our house. The clouds parted, giving way to bright sunshine. A warm breeze carried the hints of blooming honeysuckle and gardenia and seemed to induce the birds into a competitive songfest. A person just arriving in town would never suspect that just days earlier, the streets were a battlefield, and noxious gases filled the air.

To my dismay, the documents weren't in the phonebook. Harper tapped my shoulder and pointed to a young man behind the cash register holding up a brown envelope.

"You looking for this?" he asked.

Harper stared at him. "Maybe."

"I am," I said, approaching him. "Thank you."

"Mrs. Banks left it in the white pages, but it fell out after she left. I thought someone would come for it. Kind of like a spy drop, you know." He turned to Harper. "Great T-shirt."

Harper smiled. "Thanks."

I opened the envelope and looked at the first page. It was captioned "CONFIDENTIAL" and included a summary paragraph that referred to a "battle plan" of how the Soldiers of the Savior would render laws they didn't like unenforceable, ban books, and change the school curriculum to reflect Christian values. I was flipping through the rest of the document when I heard Harper clearing her throat. When I looked up, she was staring at me. "You look bothered," she said. "What is it?"

I slipped the papers back into the envelope. "Over donuts," I said. "Whatever you want."

•   •   •

The smell of freshly baked pastries preceded our arrival at the bakery. We ordered a selection of donuts, apple fritters, and pecan cinnamon rolls and took them outside, where a young man was wiping the rain off the chairs.

"Hey, Harper. I really liked your T-shirt. It was awesome."

I looked at her. "You're famous."

She smirked, then shrugged.

We took seats at a table under a maple tree that was almost in full leaf. It was Sunday morning and the church crowd hadn't arrived yet, so we had the eating area to ourselves. I suggested we eat first and deal with the contents of the envelope second. But Harper was insistent on being shown what I'd read that had, in her words, "made me cranky."

I handed her a sheet of paper. "These are the names of women the attorney general is considering charging under the abortion law. Sheila was at the top of the list."

"They want to charge other women who were raped?"

I passed her ten pages secured by a staple. "This is a legal memorandum addressed to Governor Adams and Lieutenant Governor Tanya Cobb. A group calling themselves Soldiers of the Savior prepared the memo. It presents a vision of the future in which the state controls abortion, birth control, voting rights, school prayer, education, history, marriage, and a host of other matters. In effect, there are no rights, only rules everyone must follow."

"Wait. I don't understand. How can I have no rights?"

"I'm just telling you what the governor and his friends are advocating. Around page five, the author presents a legal theory under which rape victims can be sued under the abortion law. I haven't read it thoroughly, but the gist of it is that a woman claiming she was entitled to an abortion under the rape exception has the legal burden of proving she was raped. That's a big deal, and in my legal opinion, dead wrong. The women on the list are potential defendants and will either plead guilty or have to take their chances in front of a jury. I'm sure some of them can't afford a lawyer and will have to rely on a public defender. The point is, until the last of the supreme court opinions supporting women's rights can be reversed and older state laws changed, the group is advocating that the governor makes the exercise of those rights impossible."

"So take the memo and give it to the press. Let everyone see what they're up to."

"I can't do that. They'll just deny knowledge of it or claim I wrote it. I have to catch them in the act. I'll start with the women on the list."

"Can you stop them?"

I slipped the papers into the envelope and set it on the table. "I don't know, sweetie."

"You need to read them and do what you do, you know, take notes and make up arguments."

"I can't," I said, shaking my head. "Not today. I'm just too tired." My eyes welled up. "Let's go home."

"I'm sorry, Mom." Harper's voice cracked with worry.

"Sweetie, it's okay. Please don't worry. I just need a break."

She clicked the keys on her phone and turned it toward me. A video of kittens playing with each other was running in a loop.

"How about we clean kitty boxes at Feline Friends?" she said.

For a moment, I watched the three kittens pouncing and biting.

"Shoveling cat poop sounds perfect."

CHAPTER SEVENTEEN

We dropped the pastries at home and then walked to the shelter operated by Feline Friends. The organization trapped older, feral cats and neutered and spayed them. The shelter brought kittens in to examine, socialize, and put up for adoption. Volunteers played with kittens, cleaned cages, and helped veterinarians with injured animals.

I reminded Harper we weren't going to the shelter to adopt a cat. The truth was that I was warning myself. Several times, an orphan feline had wrapped it's paws around my heart and urged me to take it to live with me. Fortunately, these kitties had homes waiting for them. But my susceptibility to a wide-eyed feline remained.

I quickly found myself engaged with a litter of kittens who treated me as a human cat tree and a perfect place to stage attacks on unsuspecting siblings. An hour later, they had regrouped on my lap into a puddle where heads and tails were distributed randomly. I stroked their soft kitten fur and was rewarded with a chorus of bubbly purrs. I carefully transferred them to a blanket, where they reassembled without waking.

I took a turn at cleaning kitty boxes and cages, then spent time with some older cats who weren't garnering the attention of the kittens. Kittens don't stay little and fluffy for long. Behind all that innocent cuteness is a cat in waiting. Older cats are harder to place in new homes because they don't appear cuddly and because their presence in a shelter raises questions about their socialization. Many times, people send an older cat to a shelter for no fault of its own. I'm partial to these kitties because I empathize with being rejected.

With some coaxing, two full-grown black and white cats allowed me to brush them. A third, an orange tabby, cowered in the back of the enclosure and hissed when I tried to pet him.

"That's okay. You're entitled to your space. I'll just sit here and we can talk or just hiss at each other."

"That's Blakely."

I turned and saw a tall man with sandy hair watching me.

"Blakely had a loving family until COVID hit. The family moved after the father died and abandoned Blakely. He's a sweetheart, but he's lost his ability to trust humans."

"I know the feeling," I said. "I'm Ashley Corbin."

"Harper's mom. Sure. Terry Logan. I'm the resident veterinarian and sometimes cat whisperer. Nice to meet you. Blakely, by the way, is watching you. I'll take him home with me tonight, but maybe you can come back next week and visit him again. I think he senses you're a cat person."

I said I'd think about it and then watched Terry leave.

"If I were older, I might hit on him," said Harper. She gave me a knowing smile. "It's okay to look."

"What? We were just talking about Blakely."

"They're closing up, and I'm hungry."

"Thank you, by the way, for getting me out of the house. I needed this as much as the cats. I just wish I could do more to help them."

"In case you're wondering, Terry's single."

•   •   •

At Harper's insistence, we ate dinner and watched a movie together. I had agreed not to look at my files or my computer, but could review a text from Eric if I received one.

Sheila's apartment was no longer considered a crime scene. Helena had requested that he pack up her things, but because he had to testify at a trial, he wasn't available. I texted back that I would be happy to fulfill her request and take Sheila's effects to Helena's ranch.

Harper read the text, then stared at me, then returned her eyes to the text.

"Hey, sweetie. You know, I don't think you look well."

She turned her head slightly, then looked at me. "Meaning what?"

"What I think you need is fresh air. Maybe a trip to the country, you know, to an alpaca ranch."

She put her hand to her head and narrowed her eyes. "I have a headache," she said with all the drama she could muster. "If I'm sick, I shouldn't be around other kids."

I explained the purpose of the trip and then gave Helena a call. She sent directions and a list of the things in Sheila's room that were the most precious and a reminder that we should wear jeans and bring or wear a pair of old shoes.

When Harper was in bed, I opened the brown envelope and read the memorandum carefully. I tried to imagine a society controlled by the likes of Tanya Cobb, a society that would deny Harper the right to be who she wanted to be. The Soldiers of the Savior and their ilk wouldn't be satisfied until they had extinguished her last rights. Like termites, they were busy doing their destructive work while most people slept. I could only hope we would all wake up in time to preserve the liberties we had once cherished.

I then turned my attention to the women on the list who were candidates for prosecution under the abortion law. All of them were rape victims. Unless I could protect them, each would be subjected to the same treatment as Sheila.

The task was daunting.

I put the documents away.

"Later," I said out loud.

CHAPTER EIGHTEEN

Monday morning, Harper and I collected boxes from the supermarket. I suggested she wait in the car while I packed the items on Helena's list, but Harper wanted no part of it. "I want to see where it happened."

Her attitude changed when we stepped into the townhouse. The rooms were as I'd left them. I don't know what Harper had expected to see, but the broken plates, toppled furniture, and smashed walls seemed to drain her curiosity. When she saw the bloody handprint on the tablecloth, she asked if she could wait outside. I took the boxes, packed them, and carried them to the car. I left her to her thoughts, and we drove away in silence.

The road to Sumner was an old two-lane that wound through the hills and mountains to the west of Freeman's Gate. We couldn't have asked for a nicer day. Sunlight filtered through newly leafed trees and dappled the road with moving light and shadows. A stream played hide-and-seek with the highway. With the windows open, the shrill voices of crickets played against the soft babble of water rushing over well-polished rocks.

Where the trees had been cleared, long-abandoned houses fought to stay vertical. One old home still had chairs on its sagging porch. Thoughts of who had lived there and what had happened to them filled my head. What ghosts lived there now? What stories could they tell about lives long forgotten?

"Are you okay?"

I turned and gave Harper a quizzical look.

"You were sighing and sniffing like you were going to cry."

I forced a laugh. "Sorry. Just allergies."

"It's pretty here," she said. "It's good to get away from…all that."

Two hours later, we arrived in Sumner. Strip malls filled with the requisite supermarkets, gas stations, fast-food outlets, and service providers lined the main road on both sides. This part of Sumner looked like other nondescript towns. But as we left the commerce district, a hay barn appeared on the right and an agricultural supply store on the left. The air was thick with the smell of livestock and feed. Harper made a disparaging "ew" and rolled up her window, but I found the smells and stores oddly satisfying.

The directions Helena provided required making turns keyed to landmarks like a red mailbox on a wooden post and a collapsed one-room school. With each turn, the road seemed to narrow, and the potholes seemed to expand. Before long, we were traveling on unpaved roads in need of grading and perhaps a load of blue stone.

After the fourth cattle guard, we kept watch for a sign for the Alpaca Ranch. According to our instructions, the sign marked a break in a barbed wire fence that was the entrance to the ranch driveway. We found the sign, but I hesitated to make the turn. With a shrug, I pulled the car onto a muddy track that meandered across the face of a hill. Harper wondered out loud whether we'd made a mistake, but a few minutes later, a large barn appeared. To my relief, I spotted a pickup truck parked in front of a small house. Three dogs were resting on the porch. As we pulled to a stop, they announced our arrival with an assortment of barks and howls.

Helena stepped out of the house and the barking stopped. She studied me for a moment. "You look beat," she said, then pointed to a rocker. "Take a seat."

She put her arm around Harper and squeezed her like she was family. A small man wearing a wide-brimmed straw hat appeared from the barn. Helena shouted at him in Spanish and he came toward us.

"This is John Jimenez. John, this is Ashley and Harper Cobin. Ashley will need help with some boxes."

"Pleased to meet you, Señora, Señorita," he said with a slight nod of his head.

"John knows everything about alpacas and their wool and how to keep me from losing my mind." She faced him, said something in Spanish again, and then turned back to me. "We'll unpack the car, and then John will give Harper a quick tour. If you're up for a short hike, I'd like to show you something."

We removed the boxes and put them in a bedroom that I was certain had once been Sheila's. The bed was made and a vase of fresh flowers adorned the nightstand next to it. I could feel the tide of sadness rising again and left the room before it could swallow me.

With the car unloaded, I followed Helena and John through a paddock where the alpacas were being fed. Harper's initial sensitivity to the smell of farm life was overcome by her fascination with a group of baby alpacas that were frolicking and butting each other.

Helena and I left the paddock and followed a path up a small hill. At its crest was a circular patio lined with benches fashioned from tree trunks. At the center of the circle was an urn and a photo encased in plastic of Sheila hugging a cat. Helena took a seat, and I sat next to her. The soft quaking of river birch leaves and the songs of insects that flittered around us enhanced the solemnity of the venue.

"You are worried about Harper," said Helena, "because you are worried about yourself. There is much to be worried about in the world today, but you feel it more than most because you seek to counter the forces that threaten your desire for equilibrium. It is an impossible task because others seek chaos. You are trying to plug a leaking dike while others are riddling it with holes, but you can't. Your desire for balance in your life keeps you trying despite the futility of the effort."

"I'm not sure I see myself that way…Equilibrium. That's a strange word choice."

Helena laughed. "I sound like an old hippie, I know, but it's the way I am. Maybe a bit too much weed or acid when I was younger, or the monk I used to live with. I spent some years at a commune, learning to meditate and read people. I guess it's presumptuous to say that. I get vibes from you and so did Sheila. She was quite fond of you."

At the sound of her name, I felt my grasp on my emotions slipping. I clung desperately to the notion that being strong meant feeling numb, but the effort was in vain. I was stunned by how quickly a wave of sadness consumed me.

I had watched as a young woman seeking a better life was destroyed by forces neither of us could control, by people who professed to love the living and killed her to prove it. I did nothing because following the rules made me powerless against those who didn't. I feared the same chaos mongers would destroy Harper or destroy me and leave her motherless.

I felt Helena's arms pressing me against her and heard her soft voice coaxing me to calm myself.

"The state plans to prosecute other women who received abortions under the rape exceptions, but I don't know how to help them."

"Maybe you can't, but you will suffer trying. I'd like to help you, but it's not my world that's out of balance."

"Equilibrium," I said through sobs, "is overrated."

Helena laughed. "And yet we seek it sometimes at our peril." She pulled away and then took my hand. "You and Harper are welcome here. Always."

I wiped my cheeks, then stood. "I need to get back."

A moment later, we embraced each other in a way usually reserved for lifelong friends. "Thank you," I said. "Thank you."

•   •   •

We were nearly at the barn when Harper came running towards us.

"There's a mother cat with a litter of kittens," she said excitedly. "They're so cute. Let me show you."

Harper led us to a pile of hay in the rear of the barn. A small gray tabby was lying on a blanket, nursing five kittens. She looked up wearily, apparently too exhausted to care about her inquisitive visitors.

"She's a stray that came here a few weeks ago," said Helena. "I've arranged for her to be spayed once she's raised her brood. Sheila loved cats."

Helena brought her hand to Harper's shoulder. "You remind me of her."

Harper flashed her a smile, then gently stroked the nursing mother.

I looked into Helena's eyes, then kissed her on the cheek. "We need to get going," I said.

Harper glared at me. "But we just got here."

"Well then, you'll both have to come back and stay a few days. How does that sound?"

Harper beamed at Helena. It sounded good to me, too.

•   •   •

Halfway home, Harper announced she was ravenous. The only place offering food was a barbeque stand that featured a platter of ribs or pulled pork, a soda, and homemade coleslaw. Neither the rustic appearance of the venue nor the cuisine pleased Harper but, given the choice of a platter of pork cooked on a grill or going hungry, she relented.

The decision turned out to be fortuitous. Harper ate her sandwich and part of mine. The owner took pity on me and brought me a small plate of ribs. I ordered a rack to go and left a big tip. Within five minutes of leaving, Harper was sound asleep.

CHAPTER NINETEEN

The next morning, I sent Harper to school with a note explaining she'd had a stomach bug but was doing better and to call my cell if she relapsed. Not wanting to sit at home alone, I went to the office. My suspension had been lifted, but my cases had yet to be reassigned to me. Daniel was a free man and untouchable under any legal theory I could muster. I had nothing to do and all the time to do it.

I pulled the list of potential abortion defendants from my briefcase and began keying the names into the state open investigations database. Each time the screen displayed the words "ACCESS RESTRICTED." The response alone told me that these women were indeed targets for prosecution and that it was only a matter of time before Tanya and her Soldiers of the Savior came after them.

According to the legal memo that accompanied the list, a woman who wanted to avail herself of the rape exception to the statute would have to prove that she was raped. The standard of proof, whether it be beyond a reasonable doubt, more likely than not, or a preponderance of the evidence, mattered little because the defendant wouldn't have the resources to present a robust defense.

But with the prosecution of Sheila and the threatened prosecution of her doctor, no healthcare provider was going to perform an abortion under the rape exception until the allegation of rape was adjudicated.

Getting a final decision in a rape case could take years, rendering the exception useless.

I focused on the "RESTRICTED ACCESS" banner that filled my computer screen. I understood that some files in the office database were off-limits, even to me. But what I hadn't considered was who could access my files and whether I could prevent stray eyes from reading my work product.

I called the number for the IT department and was greeted with the single word "Janine."

People who worked with computers, routers, and servers had a reputation—deserved or otherwise—for being prickly, introverted, and easily peeved. Whether myth or provable fact, the coldness in Janine's voice reinforced the stereotype and left me defensive.

"Hi," I said with a lilt I hoped would curry favor with the enigmatic Janine. "This is Ashley Corbin…"

"I know who you are." The detached voice convinced me I'd made a mistake, and I was about to say so when she said, "I was sorry to hear about that woman you defended. What can I do for you?"

"Thank you. I know you're busy, but I have a simple question about access to my files."

"Okay."

"I mean, do you keep a log of who might look at documents I create?"

"No, but I can run one for you. You think you got a snooper, do ya?" She chuckled. "You legal guys are either paranoid or curious. Sometimes both."

"Just wondering."

"Hang on a second." I heard the clicking of a keyboard and the word "okay" several times. "Nothing worse than someone nosing around in stuff that doesn't concern them." I heard a soft groan and a few more clicks. "Oh my. Someone with an account in the attorney general's office has accessed your files. It looks like some folks located here have also had a look. I could make your files private, but my boss will probably override whatever I set up. Might be good for a few days or a week. But if you want to be sneaky, I can arrange it so you get notified of anyone attempting to access your files going forward. My advice is to save important stuff on a flash drive and carry it with you."

"I like sneaky."

"Just so you know, your attempt to access records a few minutes ago was tagged by someone named T. Cobb. Is that who I think it is?"

"Yeah. Thanks Janine."

"One more thing. A few days ago, I was given an order to limit your access to the server but haven't gotten to it yet. I'm pretty busy, so it may take a few more days if you follow my drift."

I said I did and thanked her.

I was mulling over the consequence of Tanya et al. knowing I knew about the list of potential abortion defendants when I got an encrypted text from Nora notifying me of an emergency conference call with Francis Akins to discuss an anomaly in the data. The call was scheduled to start in ten minutes.

I logged into the conference call software. A thumbnail of Francis Akins' camera feed appeared in the upper left-hand corner of the screen. She looked impatient or annoyed. Or both. Another ten minutes passed when Nora's face filled the monitor. She offered apologies for being late, took a moment to sort through papers on her desk, and sighed.

"This will be quick, but I thought I should inform you that incorporating the rape kit data into the forensic database is on hold at the moment because of a possible anomaly. As you know, we use an offline system to test any major changes to our databases. Routinely, we sort the forensic data to look for clusters. A cluster is two or more rape kit profiles that match. Clusters indicate a repeat rapist. A large cluster indicates a possible serial rapist.

"When we added the rape kit data to the existing forensic database, the size of one of the clusters increased by one. We need to figure out why that happened and determine whether it indicates that we have a technical problem."

"What does that mean in English?" I asked.

"Well, either the existing data includes a rape committed by the serial rapist detected in the rape kit data or we have an anomaly, possibly an entry error. We are working to isolate the issue and determine what action to take. But I thought you should know where things stand."

Francis, who normally was multitasking during the video calls, was staring into her camera, a scowl on her face. "You don't have the authority to access identifying data."

"We don't and won't. Keep in mind I'm talking about data that was collected at crime scenes. These data aren't taken from arrestees. Once we find the record matching the cluster we found in the rape kit data—if there is one—we can request the case information, learn who the victim and the perpetrator are, and reveal who this serial rapist may be. It won't be today because we're booked solid, but we should be able to clear this up by the end of the week. We haven't gone live, so there is no risk our databases have been corrupted."

By the time Nora had finished, Francis was texting feverishly. A moment later, her image disappeared from the screen.

"We've poked the bear," I said.

Nora gave me a worried look. "Let's hope he doesn't bite."

The call buoyed my spirits. If the attorney general took the bait and asked about the expungement of Sheila Fanning's crime scene data, it would confirm my suspicions that Daniel was a serial rapist and that the governor or someone in his orbit knew it.

I turned off my computer and then stared at my reflection on the monitor. What I saw was a tired woman, a woman who was about to lose her job, whose daughter was only a few years from leaving home, and who, at thirty-five, was on course to live and die alone having accomplished nothing meaningful in her pathetic life.

I leaned forward and pointed at myself. "That's harsh," I said. "You owe yourself an apology." I nodded. "I'm sorry for telling you the truth." I feigned outrage. "Fuck you!"

I looked around to see if anyone had overheard my conversation with my reflection. Fortunately, it had stayed in the family.

My amusement was short-lived. I turned my attention again to the memo and the list of potential defendants. I replayed the conversation I'd had with the woman who was in charge of filtering the raw data acquired from the geofence warrants and snitch reports. What stuck in my mind was the name Phoebe Adams, the governor's daughter.

I called Janine who answered with a defensive, "I'm working on it."

"I know. I have one more little favor."

"Favors are bad enough. Little favors sound illegal and only stupid people listen to them. But then again, I'm a fan. So, what do you need?"

"Can you get me a cell phone number for Phoebe Adams?"

"Point proven," said Janine, then chuckled. "Promise me you'll tell me after I'm arrested why you want the governor's daughter's number."

"Maybe we'll share a cell."

I heard the clack of a keyboard, then Janine's voice rattling off a string of digits.

"I've got about thirty seconds to cover my tracks. Later."

I studied the number for a moment, pretending I was deciding whether to call it. With the exercise complete, I keyed in the number on my burner phone and waited. I fully expected Phoebe would screen unknown numbers and my call would roll to voicemail, but to my surprise, she picked up on the second ring.

"Hello?" she said tentatively.

"Phoebe? This is Ashley Corbin. I'm—"

"I know who you are. What do you want?"

For a moment, the question left me searching for an answer. I'd called Phoebe on a whim without considering what I'd say to her if she answered. With nothing to lose, I went with the truth.

"I'm investigating the circumstances of Sheila Fanning's arrest under the abortion law. The state's been running a program where they collect information about cell phones that spent significant time near abortion clinics. The number of one of those phones belonged to you. I'm not trying to pry, but I was—"

"Who told you that? Leave me alone."

"I didn't mean to upset you—"

"Fuck you! Don't call me again."

Phoebe's response was predictably defensive, but not totally a waste of time. She didn't deny she was visiting abortion clinics. I considered calling her back and asking her who she thought might have revealed her secret but was certain she wouldn't answer a second time.

With the call ended, I was out of ideas. Daniel Lockhart was no closer to being revealed as a rapist and the state government was still in the hands of a group from Earth-Two. I had accomplished little and still had most of the day ahead of me. I dithered between going home and bothering Martin. A call from an unknown number broke the tie.

"Who are you, and what do you want?"

"Understandably not friendly and, whether you believe me or not, I was very sad to hear about Sheila."

The voice belonged to Daniel Lockhart. I pressed the record button on my phone.

"You understand that calling me violates your restraining order? That I could have you arrested?"

"You could, but you shouldn't want to. I just want to meet somewhere public and see if we can't work out our differences in a way that would be better for you, me, and Harper."

"You terrorized my daughter and threatened us both. Having a chat won't change that."

"What if it could? What if, after we chatted like adults, I would stop blaming you for ruining my life and you would stop stalking me?"

I haven't read *The Art of War* or much of it, but I would bet if I did I'd find something like, "*If your enemy wants to reveal himself, let him.*" Daniel was right. I was stalking him. Putting him in jail was my top priority. It was time he learned just how determined I was.

"If I agree, you understand it's a temporary truce and doesn't void the restraining order."

"And you won't arrest me for calling you?"

"Meet me at the food court in the Old Town Mall."

CHAPTER TWENTY

The Old Town Mall was a collection of shops that occupied the lower floor of what had once been a tobacco barn. The mall spanned an entire block and offered entrances off Main Street and King Street. I entered from King and made my way toward the food court. I spotted Daniel pacing, glancing over one shoulder and then the other, looking like a man who was being hunted. That he was worried pleased me.

I had positioned myself behind a post when my phone signaled the arrival of an encrypted text from Nora: "Request to confirm the deletion of Sheila's evidence from the forensics file received and given."

The attorney general had taken the bait. He knew about Daniel's prior rapes. Now the question was what I was going to do about it.

I moved closer, keeping to the edge of Daniel's field of view. When he finally saw me, he froze, his eyes fixed on me in a cold stare. I could feel his anger even at a distance. He watched as I approached, then took a seat at a table farthest from the entrance of the food court.

"You said you wanted to see me. I'm here. For the record, this doesn't mean I'm waiving my rights under the protective order but agree that this meeting isn't a violation of that order. So, what do you want?"

"First, I want you to put your cell phone and your laptop on the table so I can confirm they are both powered off."

I complied and then asked to see his phone.

With the mutual lack of trust dealt with, he leaned back and locked his hands behind his head.

"What do I want? Such a simple question, but one I would gladly answer if I thought you were sincere about wanting to know." He worked his jaw, causing the muscles on the side of his face to throb. "But since you asked, I want you to leave me alone. I want you to let me disappear and be forgotten."

I feigned exasperation. "You want me to leave you alone so you can continue raping women? Is that what you're asking? Why would I do that?"

"I don't rape women. I was acquitted." When I scoffed, a big smile brightened his face. "I think we can reach an accommodation, that's why."

"You break into my house and scare my daughter and threaten me. Now you want an accommodation?"

"I didn't break in. She invited me in. I thought we discussed that."

I leaned forward and lowered my eyebrows. "Let's get something straight. I don't know you and don't care to. I don't know if you have mental problems or your mother was mean to you or a priest took advantage of you. I don't know and I don't care. What I believe is that you have been assaulting women for a long time and getting away with it. I believe you think you've gotten away with attacking Sheila, but you haven't. Not yet. Why? Because I'll never let you. Because you destroyed her life and now she's dead. So, I have no interest in cutting a deal with you today or ever."

"You destroyed my life! My life!"

The shouted remark drew the attention of others in the mall.

I rolled my eyes. "How did I do that?"

"I saved for years to build my dream home down on the river. I had everything arranged. The structure was built. It was just the interior that needed finishing. I was this close to being happy. But you charged me with rape. My money went to pay legal bills. I couldn't pay the contractors, and I couldn't get a loan. I couldn't stop the vandals from destroying my dream, and that's on you."

Daniel's face was red, and his eyes were moist and glistening. For a moment, I almost felt sorry for him. But his travails were no match for the damage he had caused. Sheila was dead and yet he saw himself as a victim? I glared at him, then pushed my chair back and began gathering my things.

He grabbed my arm. "You and your friend at the police lab have been pretty busy these last few days. You made the governor and his minions nervous about their association with me. I know you'd like to prosecute me and send me to prison, but that won't be easy, not with double jeopardy attaching to my case and all, you know, Bill of Rights stuff."

I pulled away. "Touch me again and I'll call the cops."

He raised his palms and leaned back. "Sorry."

"Is this going anywhere, or are you just blathering about how smart you are?"

"My God, you have very little patience and bad manners to boot. You owe me at least the courtesy of listening to what I have to say."

I stood. "I don't owe you anything. You raped Sheila and incited her husband to kill her. You're a serial rapist who's committed multiple assaults for which you have never been prosecuted. I don't owe you patience or manners. I owe Sheila and your other victims justice and accountability. So get over yourself."

Daniel slammed the table with his fist. "You don't talk to me that way. Not when I'm being nice." He leaned forward, then whispered. "I'm trying to show you how, with my help, you can get the governor, the attorney general, and the whole damn lot of them."

Again, eyes were drawn to where we were sitting.

I returned to the chair. "I'm listening."

Daniel closed his eyes. "You might be trying to trick me, so I'm going to offer you a hypothetical. It's just a what-if. Would that be okay?"

"I'm not into hypotheticals. Just tell me what you have to say and do it quickly."

He leaned forward, his hands clasped together and resting on the table. "I was an awkward kid. In high school, the pretty girls taunted me with their tight skirts and sweaters. They knew I could never have them. They made fun, mocked me, and humiliated me whenever they could. They were bullies and as such needed to be taught a lesson about power. What I did wasn't about sex, but about punishing my tormentors."

"So you assaulted girls, but it wasn't your fault? Even you have to know how pathetic that sounds."

Daniel glowered at me. "I do and I am…pathetic." He looked away, but his eyes were unfocused. "When I first got started, I wasn't careful and left my DNA and other evidence. Years passed and nothing happened. The rape kits from those early years were never tested and probably wouldn't be. But then there's a plan to test all the backlogged kits and put all that DNA evidence into a database." Daniel shrugged. "Even that wasn't a big deal because I had never been arrested and my DNA wasn't in the state records."

"Is there a point to this?"

"As I got older, I left those impulses behind me. I was doing fine until I encountered Sheila Fanning at the school where I taught history. I begged myself to let it pass, but I couldn't. I made a mistake."

"Sheila," I said.

"She wouldn't leave me alone. She smiled and paraded around in her skintight leggings. I tried to talk to her, but she never showed me any respect. It was as if I wasn't there. I lost control. I—"

"No, you didn't. You can't blame her. What you did is because of what your are."

"Fuck you! You don't know me."

"Tell me something I don't know or I'm leaving."

"I wasn't careful. She identified me and they found my DNA. I felt trapped. The rape kit testing would expose my past. No one would care that I was an excellent teacher and a good neighbor. They wouldn't understand why I did what I did. What was I supposed to do?" He laughed. "It all seemed hopeless. But then, it was like God was looking after me."

"Come on. Now God is helping you?"

"Scoff if you must, but you weren't there. Phillip told me that some people from the governor's office wanted to speak to me. I assumed that they already knew what I had done. Game over. But it wasn't like that."

"You're saying that you met with the governor?"

"No. Tanya Cobb, the Lieutenant Governor, and a lawyer—I don't remember his name—spoke with Phillip and me. Tanya was nice. She was the one who talked about God choosing people for important tasks. To be honest, Tanya confused me at first because I thought we were going to discuss the things I did in the past, but she just wanted to focus on Sheila's case and how sinful an abortion was. That's when I realized she didn't know about me." Daniel shook his head. "I'm afraid I'm going to jail for the rest of my life and the lieutenant governor is telling me that my case is connected to an abortion case. I didn't know Sheila was pregnant, or that she had an abortion, but I didn't care. I mean, why would I?"

"They came to you?"

"To my attorney, but yeah. Then Tanya gets to the part about how we have a common interest in me being acquitted and how there were ways to make that more likely when Phillip jumps in and insists that if I'm acquitted, he wants my DNA removed from all state databases. At that point, Phillip didn't know about my encounters with other women, so that was just something he thought of on his own. He has this thing about the government collecting information about people. All I wanted was to be acquitted before they tested the old rape kits, but then I realized I needed my data to be expunged to remain free. Don't you see how lucky I was? I had an attorney who distrusted the government. The lieutenant governor was happy to speed up my trial date. It was like God was giving me a second chance, at least until you got involved."

"When did Phillip learn about your prior rapes?"

"When you filed your first motion to delay the trial. I got worried, and he asked me why I was in such a hurry. He reminded me that whatever I told him was confidential. So I told him. He wasn't happy about it but told me he'd take care of it. He objected to your motion and kept things on track. I just needed to be acquitted."

"What about the lieutenant governor?"

"Not sure about her, but I think the attorney general realized something was off when he saw the motion for expungement. He and Phillip had quite a row about the request to erase the evidence gathered from Sheila Fanning and the schoolroom. At some point, he made the connection, but he was already too deep into helping me. Phillip told him he had to approve the motion. No one considered how persistent you are."

I sat back and tried to process how the desire to eliminate any exceptions in the abortion statute had become more important than protecting women from a serial rapist. The attorney general had moved quickly to erase any evidence of Daniel's prior rapes from state records. That overt act was a point of no return, an act that, if exposed, would end the political ambitions of anyone remotely involved.

"You still haven't told me why I should care about what happens to you."

"Because you care about Harper." He leaned toward me. "What if you found a way to arrest me for multiple rapes? What do you think I'd do? I mean, really? I expect I'll be locked up for the rest of my life, probably sodomized and beaten every day. At that point, what would I have to lose? But what if I were to promise to move away and just vanish into the backwater of humanity? Wouldn't that be better than risking everything you care about?"

"Better for whom? Sheila? How about her husband? How about the other women you assaulted, the ones who bravely reported being violently assaulted by a sexual predator? Do you know what fear they live in? How would they live knowing you were out there when you could have been locked up? The worst of it is that you're asking me to turn my back on these women in the same breath you're threatening my daughter. How does that make any sense, even to you?"

A smile crept onto Daniel's face, morphing into the smirk I despised. "You're missing the point. Even if you put me in jail and I'm off the street, the rape statistics wouldn't change. Men will rape women no matter what happens to me. And if you go around the law, the court will hold you in contempt and possibly put *you* in prison. Right now, I'm a free man. I've been tried and my DNA expunged. I can't be retried for what I did to Sheila no matter what you learn or even if I confess." He gestured at me with an extended finger. "Except you won't leave me alone," he said, his voice rising. "I don't like being bullied. I don't like being pushed around like I don't matter. If you take from me, I'll take from you. But if you agree to leave me alone, I can help you expose the governor and his supporters."

He wasn't right, but he had a point. If you have a set of values you believe in, one day you'll be tested on how important those values are. If you decide you'd rather be safe than virtuous, you have to be prepared to live with the realization you didn't believe in what you thought, or another value was more important. I made decisions, incrementally, that left Sheila dead, her husband facing a murder charge, and a serial rapist on the street. If I ceded to his threat and he raped one more woman, or a child, or a student who trusted him, that would be on me. How do I do that? How do I look at my daughter and my face in the mirror and tell myself that negotiating with Daniel was a victory of any kind? But if he carried out his threat, if he hurt Harper, how would I live with that?

"I know you're thinking about how to hurt me, but consider that I might have something you want, something to trade for leaving me alone."

"All right. What do I get for pretending you aren't a monster?"

Daniel threw up his hands. "Yes, finally, the right question. Arresting me can't possibly have the same impact as exposing the governor's office for the cesspool it is. I can give you documents— emails, texts—that might not convict him but would make the media feed like vultures. You can destroy him. That's the quid pro quo. Me for the governor and his cronies."

The Devil had made his offer. My soul—or, more accurately, my moral obligation to past and future victims of a serial rapist—in exchange for the power to expose the rot in the governor's office, to spare women the threat of prosecution under the abortion statute, and perhaps to return state politics to a more civil form of discourse.

As tempting as the Devil's offer was, accepting it would put me in the shoes of the very people I was trying to bring down. I would be the one who freed a serial rapist. I would be complicit in the death of Sheila Fanning. I would be no better than the evil I claimed to be fighting.

I felt his eyes on me, begging for my agreement, but it was not forthcoming.

"That would be a compelling trade," I said, "if I trusted you, which I don't. You need to be locked up and I will do everything I can to see you are. It might not be today or this week. You should do the right thing and tell your story about the governor and the rest of his cronies, but I won't be a party to it."

"You bitch!" His words resonated in the cavernous hall, but I was no longer listening.

"Keep in mind if you come within five hundred feet of me, my daughter, our house, or her school, I will have you prosecuted."

He bolted from his chair, joined the crowds of shoppers, and disappeared.

•　　•　　•

I sat for a few minutes while my head filled with questions I couldn't answer. I once clerked for a lawyer who told me when you have no answers and can't push your way forward, start over. Go back to the very beginning of the case or problem with no assumptions. I hated that advice because the thought of starting over sounded like an admission that I'd screwed things up from the start.

Before I unpacked my laptop, my phone buzzed.

"Hey, Eric. Funny, I was thinking I would call you. I have some news I'd like to share and a problem I can't solve alone or without a cup of expensive coffee. You game?"

He laughed. "I am, and I have a bit of news myself. Fifteen minutes. I'm buying."

·   ·   ·

I called Harper to confirm she was at school. When I told her I would pick her up, her voice filled with angst.

"What happened?"

"Nothing, sweetie. Just a precaution. I met with Daniel, and despite my good intentions managed, to upset him. You know how I am. It's a talent. Just wait with a group of kids or teachers until you see me. I'm sorry if I'm scaring you, but I'm just being really, really careful."

The call ended with Harper begging to be picked up now and me insisting she was safe in school. I heard a bell in the background and she said she had to go.

The lunch crowd was just leaving the Shade Tree Café when Eric and I arrived. We waited for a booth to be cleared of dishes and took our seats. He was smiling like a kid with a secret he couldn't wait to tell.

"You first," he said.

"I've obtained a legal memo prepared for the Soldiers of the Savior and addressed to the governor and the lieutenant governor. The document outlines a troubling political agenda, but more to the point, it lists other women who are going to be tried, just like Sheila. I'm working on contacting them but haven't gotten very far. More importantly, I just met with Daniel Lockhart and he admitted he's a serial rapist and the governor, the lieutenant governor, and the attorney general all took overt steps to cover it up."

Eric gave me an astonished look. "Holy crap. Can you prove it?" He tilted his head. "That's the problem you can't solve."

"Your news."

"I've resigned from the police department effective at the end of the month. I'm going to do something different."

"Like what?"

He shrugged. "All my options are open. But I can't do this anymore, not with the clowns running the circus." He smiled. "I was thinking I might do some traveling while I consider my options."

A waitress arrived and looked at us with a hint of a smile that barely concealed her suspicion that we were more than just friends. "The usual?"

"Sure," I said, "but double the whipped cream."

"About your problem."

I gave Eric a summary of the conversations with Phoebe and Daniel.

"You called the governor's daughter? That was gutsy."

"She was on a list of women whose phones were tracked to clinics that perform abortions."

He stared at me for a moment. "Not surprising. What do you know about her?"

I shrugged. "Not much. She and her dad don't get along. She's a bit wild. Just what's online."

"I have friends on the governor's security detail. Being assigned to watch Phoebe is considered punishment. She's more often stoned than sober and can be belligerent on a good day. When she acts out, it's the security team that gets the blame."

"That sucks."

"Some news junkie made a video of her misbehaving at a bar. The video showed her screaming how much she hated her father and making little gun gestures with her fingers. The video went viral, and the governor fired the security team. Even so, most of the guys feel sorry for her. When the public isn't watching, the governor berates her. Once he grabbed her by the throat so hard, an agent had to intervene. That agent was fired, too."

"Any particular reason the governor is so cruel?"

Eric smirked. "You want rumor or gossip?"

"Just tell me."

"When Phoebe was seventeen, she got pregnant. A doctor at an abortion clinic offered to help but wanted assurances he wouldn't be prosecuted. Her dad refused. Getting pregnant was her fault, and she could deal with the consequences. She dealt with it by paying a student nurse for a botched abortion. Phoebe is lucky to be alive. But the governor never forgave her for putting his political career at risk."

I clenched my teeth. "That's the man who wants to tell me and all the mothers in the state how to raise our daughters?"

"That leaves your conversation with Daniel. You have a way of pissing him off."

"Certainly appears that way. But I think I could get him to turn on the governor and his associates if I could charge him with a crime that allows me to take a new DNA sample. The problem is, I don't know what that crime would be. I'm sure if I can expose him, he'll expose the others. No way he's going down alone. But I need a crime."

I took my laptop from my bag and slid it onto the table. "All this started with the expungement motion. I know it by heart, but maybe I missed something. I don't know. Maybe I didn't, and the problem is a nut I can't crack."

The cappuccinos arrived, along with a bowl of whipped cream. The waitress gave us another congratulatory smirk and departed.

"You know, when I was younger, I might have hit on you."

I laughed. "I might have hit back. I don't know if I remember how."

"Well, get out more and fix that. You are denying someone—guy, gal—a wonderful companion."

"You make me sound like a shelter cat itching for a home. Actually, that's not too far off."

We sipped and slurped and made noises of satisfaction. "This is better than sex," I said.

Eric laughed. "Did I mention getting out more?"

"After I deal with Daniel, I'll be looking for a new job and maybe a new town. A new start. Maybe something more gratifying than chocolate milk and coffee."

"Then let's deal with him so we can get on with things."

I lifted my cup. "To new starts."

Eric tapped my cup with his. "Indeed."

I grabbed my computer. "Most of my notes deal with the rape statute and the cases that interpreted the statutory language, or in which the defendant won on appeal. The rape law was amended a few times to accommodate the introduction of DNA evidence. I have the statute of limitations and the legislative history, but nothing in my trial folder is going to help."

I put my hands behind my head and rubbed my neck. "Daniel gets off because the jury and judge were tampered with, maybe not criminally, but enough to tilt the scales in his favor. Sheila is prosecuted under a zombie law that's been on the books for decades and was only revived because of the *Dobbs* decision."

"Remind me again what a zombie law is."

"When the supreme court of the state or at the federal level rules a law unconstitutional, it can't be enforced. It should be repealed, but most legislatures don't bother. The law is dead but can be reanimated, like a zombie. Some laws still on the books make it a crime to kiss a woman below the neck or to water your lawn on Sunday."

"So, he had consensual sex at the high school. Can't you charge him with trespass or damaging public property?"

"Creative thinking. Not likely to get that past the AG, not to mention it looks petty."

Eric laughed. "In the old days, Sheila's husband could have shot Daniel for damaging *his* property. Adultery was a crime enforceable by the husband, but not the wife. Are you familiar with the famous case of Daniel Sickles?"

I stared at him blankly. "Maybe it's not as famous as you think."

"Sorry, I'm a Civil War junkie. The gist of the story is that just before the war broke out, Sickles' young wife, Teresa, was having an affair with Phillip Key, the son of Francis Scott Key. Sickles, then a congressman from New York, was a known womanizer. He suspected his wife of adultery, but she denied it and he believed her. But then, someone sent Sickles a letter confirming her cheating, and he made her sign a confession. The story is that Sickles saw Key on a bench outside the Sickles' residence and shot him. Key wasn't armed and Sickles was charged with murder. But he beat the rap, claiming temporary insanity but also arguing that his wife's infidelity gave him the right of self-defense. If I remember correctly, Sickles argued Key had disrupted the sanctity of his home and that Sickles was defending his property. The court took a dim view of a woman who committed adultery. Not so the husband."

I looked at him frozen-eyed, but didn't speak.

"What? You're either having a stroke or some kind of eureka moment. Which is it?"

"Maybe both. I've been so focused on how the law of consent applied to Sheila that I didn't consider how the law would view Daniel's conduct, assuming the sex was consensual. He admitted to adultery."

I brought the expungement motion up on my computer and stared at it while Eric stared at me.

"How about sharing?"

"This is the from the expungement order: '…all DNA derived from the person of Sheila Fanning, her clothing, and the place of the consensual sexual activity between her and Daniel Lockhart shall be…'"

Eric shrugged. "He's admitting to having sex with her. So what?"

"She was married."

"So?"

I tapped a few keys and then turned the laptop so Eric could see the screen.

"Tell me what I'm looking at."

"In 1885, the legislature made voluntary sexual intercourse between a married person—male or female—and another person who is not that person's spouse a crime. It's not only a crime for the married person but also for the other person involved, even if that person is not married. That is the law of adultery and it's a felony. Daniel admitted to having consensual sex with Sheila Fanning while she was married to Quinn. That's adultery, and it's still a crime. Daniel Lockhart can be charged and arrested for criminal adultery."

"That can't be still on the books."

"It is." I spun the computer around and did a quick search. "Let's see. The governor asked to have it repealed in 1916 when a maid caught him fooling around with the lieutenant governor's oldest daughter, blah blah. The temperance league objected and the repeal of the statute was tabled. Some more blah blah."

I scrolled down the screen and then laughed.

"This is a fun fact. The mother of the girl the governor was shacking up with shot him but escaped liability on the grounds of temporary insanity and because everyone agreed the lech deserved it. It appears her lawyer knew about Sickles and his defense. Anyway, the consensus of the governor's advisors was that any campaign to repeal the statute would keep the sordid story in the press and the effort was dropped and forgotten." I laughed gleefully. "It's still the law, and it's a felony."

Eric smiled at me. "Another zombie law. You learn something every day. So, what are you thinking?"

"The evidence in Sheila Fanning's rape case could support a new charge of adultery," I said, "but the expungement order would be used to challenge the arrest and we'd be back where we started. I think we need to arrest him and get a new sample. We have his confession, which is enough to charge him with criminal adultery under the old statute."

Eric motioned to the waitress and held up two fingers, then turned to me. "Judge Rennick handled Sheila's bail hearing. He's also a friend of mine. He might be sympathetic to issuing an arrest warrant on an old statute."

"Before we do anything, we have to agree to keep this between us. I think my work files are being accessed by someone in the attorney general's office. For all I know, so is my laptop."

"A bit paranoid, but I'm game."

"I can prepare the arrest warrant offline or at the library, but then the system will automatically enter it into the court's electronic docket. We will have to time his arrest so we can take a DNA swab and get it to

Nora and tested before the attorney general can attempt to squash the warrant."

Eric leaned forward. "What about protecting Harper? You might get Daniel's DNA, but he won't be remanded to jail, not for adultery. Officially, he has no prior record. He'll be out on bail until we can run his DNA against the rape kit data. That's enough time for him to come after you."

"I'll call Nora. You talk to the judge. I'll figure out what to do with Harper."

"You sure you want to do this?"

"You betcha."

CHAPTER TWENTY-ONE

The plan seemed simple enough to work, but with so many moving parts and hidden agendas, it was imprudent to be overly confident. I returned to the office and found an envelope on my chair. In it, I found pages listing computers that had accessed the files I'd created to prepare for Daniel's rape trial. What was most disturbing was that attorneys who weren't involved in the case had read the files before the trial.

At the end of the log was a note: "A file used by your email client to store sent and received emails was also accessed. I have secured your email and folders, but I'm sure it will only be temporary. I need to scan your laptop for spyware. Janine."

I called her and asked her how long a scan would take.

"An hour unless I find something. I'm sure I will. Your files are really popular."

"If I wanted to download a form, can you make it so no one can know about it?"

"Sure. Let me set up a dummy account. You can load the forms to a flash drive. When you're done getting what you need, let me know and I'll delete it. I'll be up in a few minutes."

The last thing I needed was a cup of coffee, but with little to do, I headed to the kitchen, inserted a coffee pod into the machine, and hit the brew button.

When I returned, Janine was at my desk. I had imagined her as a young woman with long hair. To my surprise, she looked to be in her mid-fifties, athletic and tan, with straight silver-white hair. She must have noticed my reaction.

"Yup. Expecting the stereotypical computer geek, were ya? Well, sorry to disappoint, but I've been doing this since I was your age or thereabouts. Even had my own company, but the nerds smoked too much dope and watched too much porn. Not much more enchanted with legal types, but I admire your efforts to help Sheila. It's none of my business, but I hope all this cloak and dagger is because you're going after the ones responsible for her death. All of 'em."

She stood and handed me a yellow sticky and a flash drive. "I've set you up as Roger Rabbit and written the passcode on this sticky. You can only use it once. Save what you need on this drive and you should be good. I'll be back with your laptop as soon as I can."

The process for obtaining an arrest warrant requires a police officer to file a complaint that includes a detailed description of the crime to be charged and a written declaration showing probable cause. The officer is also required to make a sworn oral declaration of probable cause in the presence of the judge or by telephone. Except for the oral declaration, the requirements were enumerated in a form. Given that we had a confession from Daniel that he'd committed adultery, completing the warrant would only take a few minutes.

I downloaded the form onto the flash drive. I tasted the coffee, then spit it back into the cup. A moment later, I sent an encrypted text to Eric and Nora asking if they could take part in a meeting at six thirty at my house. Nora responded with a question mark, followed by the word "teleconference?"

I was eager to pick up Harper, but first, I had to sound out Martin about my plan without letting him know what it was.

His door was open, his attention focused on his computer. He didn't look up but motioned me in. I leaned against the doorjamb and stayed put. After a moment, he muttered the word "damn" and shook his head. "State's leading scorer twisted his ankle last night and may not be ready for the tournament. I stand to make a killing if he plays. Without him, State is doomed. What's going on with you?"

"I met with Daniel Lockhart this afternoon. He said some interesting things, some of which might even be true."

Martin looked at me, then pursed his lips. "Hard to know what to believe or who to trust these days."

"You threw me under the bus."

"That bus was going to hit you regardless of what I did, but I understand why you might still be annoyed with me."

"Daniel was convinced that I was trying to tie him to a string of rapes committed some time ago. He offered to expose the governor, the attorney general, and others in manipulating his trial to guarantee an acquittal so they could then try Sheila Fanning for an illegal abortion."

Martin leaned back in his chair. "I would ask if you took the deal, but I guess that's where we bump into the trust line."

"It's not a deal I'm authorized to make, even if I could tie him to other rapes. I'm pretty sure if it were up to me, I would want to nail both the governor and Daniel."

"Then that's what you should do."

"And if I needed help?"

"You'd have to find someone you trust, someone who wouldn't betray you, someone you believe has your best interest at heart."

"Good to know. Thank you."

Janine appeared. "I think I found the problem on your computer. Let me show you."

I thanked Martin and followed Janine back to my office. "You had a bot that captured your keystrokes. I found the same bot on Martin's computer last week. What I couldn't determine is who was reading what you were typing."

"It wasn't Martin?"

She pulled her head back and scowled. "No. Of course not. I ran the same sweep of his files and his laptop. Same results. As I told him, I recommend you use a VPN at home and run this program on all your personal devices."

I spent the next few minutes filling in the arrest warrant form and another ten finding texts and statements Daniel had made showing he knew Sheila was married. Those statements and the admission in the expungement motion would be enough to establish probable cause for his arrest under the criminal adultery statute.

I texted Martin the invitation to the meeting at my house and immediately received a one-word reply: "Insurrection?" followed by a thumbs-up emoji.

I slipped my laptop into my briefcase and then surveyed my office. I was gripped by an odd mix of melancholy and excitement, akin to the feeling I had when I left home for college. I didn't know what the future held for me then or now, but I'd made the decision to go after Daniel and there was no turning back.

CHAPTER TWENTY-TWO

Harper was waiting for me in the parking lot that fronted her school. When we stopped at Thai Magic, she gave me a suspicious look.

"Either you have good news and we're celebrating or something bad has happened and you're trying to soften the blow. Which is it?"

"Two things can be true at the same time. You'll like part of it and the rest not so much."

She folded her arms across her chest and glared at me.

"I've invited some of my colleagues over to discuss some things; you're invited to join and speak your mind. Until then, let's get through dinner."

I set the bags on the kitchen counter and motioned for her to sit. "I'm not eating until I know what you're up to."

I puffed my cheeks. "You're too young to be so goddamned stubborn. Why you had to acquire my worst traits is beyond me."

I opened a bottle of wine, filled a glass, and sat across from her.

"I have the option of reinventing myself and moving on. All I have to do is forget what happened to Sheila and let Daniel Lockhart live his life."

"You can't…"

I held up both hands. "Stop and try to just listen for two minutes. I can't, and I won't. In some ways, it would be a relief to accept defeat, but, because your mother isn't just smart and reasonably attractive for her age—*and* a bad loser—I have a plan that, if successful, would take care of all the slime balls in the governor's office and Daniel."

Harper smiled. "I like it when I take after you. So, why is that bad news?"

"Because it's dangerous. Daniel has threatened me—us—and the political machine behind the governor won't give up without a fight. Wanting to do good things is fine, but doing them comes at a cost, especially when things don't go the way you want. In this case, the risk can't be measured. The folks that are coming tonight will help determine what those risks are and whether they can be mitigated sufficiently to proceed."

"How dangerous?"

I shrugged but didn't answer the question.

"So, you'll discuss my future while I sit in my room?"

"No, sweetie. We're in this together. You'll get to speak your mind. But understand this. I won't let any plan go forward unless I can protect you. That isn't up for discussion, debate, or negotiation. If you don't like your options or mine, that ends it. Are we good?"

Harper nodded.

"Let's eat while the food is hot," I said.

•   •   •

An hour later, I established a video conferencing link with Nora and projected her video onto the wide-screen TV. She held up a glass of what I guessed was whiskey, then took a seat on a sofa. Eric arrived shortly thereafter. Harper greeted him at the door with a big hug. Martin was next and accepted a beer.

With the conspirators assembled, it was time to set things in motion. We ushered everyone into the living room, where I introduced Nora. Eric took a moment to perform a cursory search for listening devices but found none.

The search drew a worried look from Nora. "You're scaring me," she said, then drained her glass. "I need a refill."

"Just being cautious." I handed each of the attendees a yellow sticky and showed it to Nora. "This is the number of a phone you should use to contact me going forward."

"You have a burner phone?" asked Harper.

I smiled.

"That's like cool and scary at the same time."

"The reason we're here is that I'm convinced Daniel Lockhart is a serial rapist, the governor's political machine knows it and has known it, and in exchange for his silence about monkeying with the jury at Daniel's rape trial, were willing to let him go free."

"Can you prove those allegations?" asked Martin.

"Not in a court controlled by the governor, and maybe not at all. But I don't have to. Daniel confessed as much to me earlier today. I'm not here to debate those facts but to discuss what might be done legally to expose Daniel's past crimes. If he gets locked up, I'm sure he'll turn on his facilitators."

I walked through the warrant I'd drafted to charge Daniel with criminal adultery and arrest him.

"Seriously," said Nora. "It's a crime in this state to screw your friend's husband even if you're not married?" She glanced at Harper. "Sorry. I get potty-mouthed when I drink."

"It's not just a crime but a felony," I said, "and that qualifies Daniel for another DNA test. Once we take his sample, we will need to get it to the lab for processing on an expedited basis. The attorney general will try to block anyone from using Daniel's DNA, so we have to expedite comparing his DNA to the rape kit data. That's where Nora comes in. After that, Eric will arrest Daniel again and this time, he'll be locked up without bail."

I studied the faces of my coconspirators. All but Martin seemed to accept the plan as I'd stated it. He was staring into space, his fingers laced together, his hands pressed to his lips. This was his worry pose, and it worried me.

"What is it, Martin?"

"I know you're in a hurry and for good reason, but you have to follow standard procedure. You can't expedite everything because that means you're treating Daniel selectively. You could win the battle and lose the war on appeal. If you want to get a quick turnaround on his DNA, you have to comply with the protocols that allow for that. Keep in mind a trial judge or an appellate judge will only see Daniel's record, which, after his expungement motion, is clean."

"That will take time," said Eric. "Daniel won't face incarceration on the adultery charge. Until we get the DNA match, he'll be a free man and will look for retribution. That also allows the attorney general to file a ton of paperwork with the court to protect the governor. I don't like it."

I turned to Nora. "Assuming we follow protocol, what is the usual time to get a DNA sample tested and searched against the forensic database?"

"A couple of days for a major crime, but I can't guess how we would prioritize adultery. That could be days or weeks."

"Daniel has threatened Ashley and Harper," offered Eric. "That's a lot of time to provide security." He turned to Harper. "What do you think? Don't say what you think we want to hear."

Harper looked at me, and then at the other adults in the room. "I want him to pay for what he did to Sheila. But he scares me. I don't know what you want me to say."

"What if you could go somewhere safe for a few days?" replied Eric.

"As long as it isn't with my grandparents."

"Oh sweetie, I wouldn't do that to you, ever," I said, then turned to Eric. "What do you have in mind?"

"I spoke with Helena this afternoon to update her on things. She offered to let Harper stay with her."

Harper was stunned. "I can skip school to hide out on her alpaca ranch?"

Eric nodded.

"That'd be cool. I'd like that. And next week is spring break. That's like almost two weeks."

"You'll be doing your schoolwork remotely," I said.

Harper rolled her eyes. "Sure, Mom."

"That leaves Nora and Ashley," said Martin.

"I've got security cameras everywhere," said Nora, then lifted her sweater, revealing a holster and the grip of an automatic. "I don't know if I could shoot someone, but they don't know that."

"I know some guys who can provide security for Ashley," said Eric, then turned to me. "We were going to install webcams after Daniel's visit. Did you order them?"

"On my list," I said, then handed copies of the draft warrant to Martin and Eric. "I'll drive Harper to Helena's ranch tomorrow. Hopefully, we can have Daniel arrested by tomorrow evening. That's when the clock starts."

Eric helped me pick out security cameras, and I ordered them with overnight delivery. He agreed he would come by while I was driving Harper to Helena's ranch and install them.

After he left, I spent an hour on the phone with Helena explaining what the plan was, why it might not work, and what the risks were. She asked to speak with Harper. I could hear my daughter's animated voice as Helena summarized what life on an alpaca ranch was like. I heard her say, "For sure, I'll earn my keep," followed by a pause and then, "Yes, ma'am. I have jeans but not boots or gloves, but we can get them in town. Okay. Okay." She handed me the phone, and left with the words, "I need to pack."

With the arrangements made, I set an alarm and went to bed early. Sleep is a fickle friend, and as often as I drifted into slumber, the image of Daniel Lockhart's smug, sneering smile jolted me awake.

I took solace in knowing that tomorrow I was going to wipe that grin off his face—permanently.

CHAPTER TWENTY-THREE

When the alarm signaled it was time to get up, I was exhausted. I poured a cup of coffee before it had finished brewing, spilled it on the floor, and vented my frustration loud enough to bring Harper out of her room in a panic. She was dressed, bright-eyed, and eager to leave. She offered to make the coffee again if I would leave the room, take a shower, and return with my head on straight. Sometimes, it's hard to tell who the parent is in this house.

When I returned to the kitchen, Harper was sitting at the table, staring into a bowl of cereal. She faced me, frowning. "I'm not going. Helena called and said a storm had turned the roads to mud and they were impassable. It's not fair."

I sat across from her. "I'm sorry, sweetie. It isn't fair."

She looked at me through worried eyes. "I'm afraid of what Daniel might do to you if you arrest him. Maybe it would be better if you just let him go."

"If that's what you want."

Harper got up without eating. "I don't want anything. Is it okay if I get ready for school?"

I watched her walk away. A moment later, she reappeared.

"Arrest him and lock him up so he'll never get out," she said. "That's what I want."

•　　　•　　　•

I conveyed the news about Helena to Eric. He arrived shortly thereafter.

"If you want to call off filing the arrest warrant, no one is going to judge you for it. If we go forward, it's a complication that we will need to deal with. Your call."

I told him that Harper wanted us to proceed with the plan. He agreed to drop her off at school, leaving me alone to wonder if I'd made the right decision. An hour later, I received a text from Eric confirming the filing of the arrest warrant. We had pushed the first domino. The next move was up to the judge.

I spent the morning puttering around the house and looking at my phone. Around ten, I received a notification that the security cameras had arrived. I took some time to unpack them and peruse the installation instructions. After reading them twice, I lost interest, tossed all the devices back into the box, and put them on the dining room table where Eric would see them.

I received a message from Martin containing a link to the warrant authorizing the arrest of Daniel Lockhart for criminal adultery. Eric texted that he, Martin, and another officer had arrived at Daniel's house, arrested him, taken a sample, and allowed him to call his attorney. The judge who'd issued the warrant was standing by to arraign Daniel. I was told to meet them at the courthouse in an hour.

I could wait at home or in the courthouse. Choosing the latter, I headed out. I was outside the courtroom when Phillip Dunlevy approached me. "I thought I was tenacious," he said, "but you're one determined lady."

"If you meant bitch, you could have said so. Actually, it would be a compliment coming from you. Anyway, what are you doing here? He said he was going to represent himself."

"I felt sorry for him, so now I'm going to defend him one more time. Oddly, I feel a little sorry for you, too."

I laughed. "You don't feel sorry for anyone. What are you getting at?"

"Finding an old law to charge him with was clever, but you know it's just a temporary victory. The clerk forwarded the arrest warrant to the attorney general. He's been busy cutting your legs out from under you."

"Meaning what?"

Before Phillip could respond, Daniel appeared. Eric had a hand on Daniel's arm. As they came closer, I could see that Daniel's hands were cuffed.

He stared at me, his face a mask of hatred and suppressed rage.

Phillip greeted him with a quick, "Don't say anything," and then demanded that Eric remove the handcuffs.

"When we're in front of the judge," said Eric.

The proceeding was brief. Daniel acknowledged he understood the charges, pleaded not guilty, and was released without bond. Before he could depart the courtroom, Phillip asked if we could all meet in a conference room.

The conference room featured a large table, but no one sat. Phillip and Daniel stood near the door while Eric, Martin, and I took positions at the other end of the room.

Phillip closed the door, but before he could speak, Daniel charged me. "I warned you. I told you what would happen if you came after me."

Eric stepped in front of him, and he backed away.

"Daniel," said Phillip. "Let me handle this."

Phillip handed Martin a paper. "It appears this little game was for nothing," he said. "The attorney general has suspended the enforcement of the adultery statute. He has also ruled that the DNA data from the rape kit testing program doesn't meet state standards and is to be discarded. It isn't clear if the state will retest the kits. Regardless, I will move to quash the warrant and have Daniel's latest DNA sample destroyed. Later today, I will file a civil action seeking damages for malicious prosecution."

"The attorney general doesn't have the authority to suspend a law," I said.

Phillip shrugged. "Maybe not, but by the time you litigate it, it won't matter."

"You'll pay for this!" screamed Daniel. "I warned you. You'll pay."

Phillip grabbed Daniel's arm and pulled him out of the conference room.

Eric, Martin, and I stood silently for a moment, stung by our defeat.

"Can the attorney general just decide what data is good and what the law is?" asked Eric.

"Probably not, but it doesn't matter," said Martin. "At some point, we have to recognize we're fighting an asymmetric battle. We play by the rules and the governor makes them up as he goes along. Unless that changes, we are always going to be outmaneuvered. What we have to deal with now is whether Daniel is going to make good on his threats."

"I'll send someone to Harper's school," offered Eric. "She'll be fine."

"She'll be fine today," I said, "but what about tomorrow or next week? This is my fault, and I'm clueless about how to fix it."

"Go home and wait for me," said Eric. "Just let me handle this."

•   •   •

I was at the door when Eric arrived with Harper. She stepped around me, went to her room, and slammed the door.

"I told her what went down at the courthouse. She doesn't get how someone like Daniel can be free and she's a prisoner in her own house. My advice is to let her stew a bit and come to her own conclusion. We still don't know how dangerous Daniel is. There's always the option of just shooting him."

"Good to have options," I said.

"Actually, we have plenty of them."

"Meaning?"

"They sped up my retirement, so I'm officially off the police force. I'm badgeless and gunless for the first time in over thirty years. You and Martin have been fired, although Martin told me the attorney general doesn't have the authority to fire either of you. He said he will sue him."

"I thought it was a good plan," I said with a shrug. "Apparently not. I was just reinstated yesterday. Now what do I do?"

"Sit tight? Look for a job? Get fat drinking cappuccinos? I don't know."

"We kicked the hornet's nest and for what? This is my doing. I made a mess of things. Not just my life, but Harper's, too."

Eric squeezed my shoulder. "Until I think of something else, the new reality is that Daniel is free, and he's pissed. He might just decide to leave, but he might not. We need to plan for the worst. I have to take care of a few things tonight, but tomorrow afternoon I'll come over and install your cameras. Lock the door after I leave and call me if something seems off."

I spent the evening hoping to see Harper emerge from her room and feeling increasingly guilty when she didn't. I went to bed convinced I'd ruined her life and put her at risk for nothing. I'd failed her as a mother, and no amount of rationalizing would change that.

CHAPTER TWENTY-FOUR

The next morning, I found Harper's dishes in the sink. She was sitting in the kitchen scrolling through social media posts. Her pretty eyes were puffy and marked by dark circles. I looked at her, tears rolling down my cheeks, and begged her to forgive me.

She looked at me, her lower lip trembling. "It's not your fault; it's mine. I made you do this. I made you fight back and now Daniel is going to kill you."

"No, sweetie. You can't think like that. He isn't going to kill me."

"You don't know what he's going to do. I can't live like this. Tell me that people like Governor Adams and that awful Tanya woman will never be in charge of my life. If you can't, I want to move somewhere where being a girl isn't a crime."

I sat next to her and closed my eyes. "At this moment, I don't know how to fight them. I'm tired and out of ideas and if I had an idea, I'd probably think twice about telling anyone. But we're in this together. Okay. You and me. Let's get through the next few days. Then we can figure out our future."

•   •   •

After driving Harper to school, I went back to bed and slept hard. It was a little after ten when my burner phone made a sound like breaking glass, which indicated a call from Eric.

"Tell me the world has come to its senses or just lie to me."

Eric laughed. "It hasn't and I'm not a good liar. How about just the facts?"

"I used to love facts. Now I'm not so much a fan. Go ahead. Ruin my day."

"Daniel has been on social media most of the night, mostly talking about how you're stalking him and how he's been mistreated. He's not overtly threatening you, but he verbally abused the governor and the lieutenant governor."

"Tanya? Why would he be mad at her?"

"He didn't say what the issue was, only that he thought they were friends and now she won't return his calls. He says she used him and owes him. What she owes him, he didn't say. His last rant was about staying in town and not letting the liars and woke peddlers win."

"Do you think he's dangerous?" I asked.

"He's a coward, but it's hard to say what he might do if cornered. I doubt he'd confront someone he thinks might hurt him, but he's living a different reality now. Even though he was acquitted, people aren't buying his respected teacher and community leader act. What is hard to determine from his posts is whether he's angrier with his former political friends or you."

"When I spoke to him at the mall, it sounded like he was blackmailing the attorney general and lieutenant governor. He's still a threat to them. I'm curious what they might do to him."

"Not our problem," said Eric, "but you need to be careful until this shakes out. I'll stop by later and install the cameras."

My phone buzzed. "Nora's calling. Stay in touch."

I pressed the answer button. "Please tell me you're all right."

"Depends on how you define all right. I'm physically fine if that's what you mean, but I'm a mess mentally, and before you ask, I'm not thinking of shooting myself and even if I were, it's not your fault. I'm calling to let you know I filed a claim under the state's whistleblower statute. My lawyer has scheduled a press conference that's going to go live in a few minutes. I just wanted to give you a heads-up."

"What whistle are you blowing, exactly?"

"That the governor, lieutenant governor, and the attorney general illegally interfered with the operation of the state crime lab for political purposes in suspending the release of the rape kit data."

"Damn, Nora. Are you sure you want to do that? I mean, that's asking for a lot of grief."

"My job is to help find criminals and put them in jail. If I just stay quiet while they suppress the rape kit data to protect Daniel Lockhart, I've wasted my career. My lawyer tells me I've got a good case. And I've signed up for gun training."

"Who's your lawyer?"

"Gene del Fero. He represents some of the women who sued the state to have their rape kits tested."

"Gene is a kind of a rock star. How—"

"He called me after the bullshit news broke about the rape kit DNA testing being flawed and offered his services for free. I won't release the data but will make public an analysis demonstrating that multiple serial rapists could be identified by the data if the lab was allowed to do its job. Anyway, Gene said I should let you know."

"What about Sheila's data that was included in the expungement order?"

"It's all on the table."

I thanked her and expressed my admiration for her courage in coming forward.

I poured the rest of the coffee, reheated it, and texted Harper about Nora's whistleblower complaint. She texted me back a thumbs up. She still wasn't engaging me about how I'd messed up her life and, for the moment, that was fine with me.

I turned on the news and tried to focus my attention on what I was going to do for employment. The subject alone was distracting, in part because it involved deciding where I was willing to move. I wasn't sure what area of the law interested me, if any. The TV chirping in the background prevented me from focusing on my future, but I didn't want to miss any news about Nora or Daniel. To my relief, the decision was made for me.

A "breaking news" banner filled the television screen, followed by a live shot of Nora and Gene del Fero answering questions. The anchor quickly reported what Nora was alleging about interference by the governor's office with the state crime lab and then cut live to the news conference.

Nora's decision to seek whistleblower status threatened to expose the corruption within the governor's political machine and could eventually reveal Daniel Lockhart as a serial rapist. Even with an excellent lawyer, the process was going to be protracted and nasty. All I could do was wait to see how it was going to shake out, but it gave me hope.

The governor's office promised to provide a comment once they had thoroughly reviewed the whistleblower filing, but they were confident that the filing was the "ranting" of a "disgruntled" employee.

The whistleblower complaint rattled Daniel. He was back on social media complaining that I was persecuting him because I couldn't accept that he'd been acquitted and because I was a failure as a lawyer. For reasons that weren't clear, he also attacked Phillip Dunlevy, his lawyer, who Daniel was convinced was plotting to betray him. Curiously, Daniel's reaction to the press conference was directed at Phillip and me despite our having nothing to do with Nora's complaint.

To my surprise, I received a copy of the filing directly from Gene del Fero. I was stunned by how detailed the disclosure was regarding the circumstances leading up to the attorney general's decision to suspend the rape kit testing program. I was also pleased that the filing challenged the decision to expunge Sheila Fanning's forensic information.

The filing had brightened my mood and triggered my appetite. I looked through the refrigerator for something to eat, preferably something sweet and decadent. Sitting behind a bag of stale bagels, I found a foam container. I opened it slowly, unsure of what it was or might have been or how old it was. To my delight, the package revealed a cinnamon pecan sticky roll. I sniffed it, then poked it. It was still soft. Smiling, I took my treasure to the microwave and heated it alongside what remained of my coffee. I could feel my endorphins rising just inhaling the aroma of nuts and sugar and cinnamon. And for a moment, the machinations of the outside world faded away.

•   •   •

I was savoring the last bite when the doorbell chimed. A week ago, I wouldn't have given it any thought. Now, the chiming reminded me I needed to install the doorbell camera. I opened the door a crack and saw a young woman dressed in a black leather jacket over a black shirt and jeans, her head covered by a short fuzz of blue hair. A gold ring hung from her nose and a smaller one looped through her right eyebrow. I recognized her as Phoebe Adams, the governor's only child.

I stared a moment longer than was polite and tried to make up for it by smiling broadly and adopting a cheery tone.

"Hi. Phoebe, right? How can I help you?"

She looked past me, her eyes unfocused, and then seemed to recover. "I shouldn't have come here. Maybe I should go."

"No. Please. Come in. I want to apologize for calling you. Can I get you something?"

She shook her head, then stepped into the foyer. "No, thank you." She peered into the living room. "Is Harper here?"

"Harper? No, she's at school. Do you know her?"

Phoebe laughed. "Not personally. I follow her on social media. She had that awesome T-shirt and interview on CNN."

"Her shirt said something about aborting your father. You find that awesome?"

She nodded. "It sent a message about my dad that I thought was on point."

I led her into the kitchen. "Have a seat while I get coffee."

Phoebe nodded but looked away, then seemed to catch herself. "If I'm acting weird, I'm sorry," she said. "I'm on a new medication for depression. I'm nineteen years old, and I have to be medicated to feel normal, whatever the hell that means." She pointed to her head. "You can look at me and see there's something loose up there. But since I can't remember what normal feels like, I have no way of knowing whether it's working or making me worse. To be honest, I hope this *isn't* normal."

"Well, if it makes you feel any better, you don't seem weird to me. I see you expressing yourself in a way I wouldn't, but that makes you you and not me."

"You're patronizing me, but I get it. Some people aren't so nice. Harper is a lucky girl." She sat at the table and I sat opposite her.

"Your call pissed me off." She whispered as if she were talking to herself. "Thinking about my experiences at the abortion clinics is enough to set me off, and then you call and start asking me about it."

"I'm sorry. That was rude and—"

"How do you know about my abortion!? Did my father tell you or was it that fat cow Tanya?" Phoebe raised her hands. "My bad for yelling. My shrink told me I raise my voice because it makes me feel tough, the same with my blue hair and black clothes. The truth is, I'm scared most of the time. Maybe worried is a better word. The world … the world scares me."

"Your phone number was on a list. Apparently, the governor and his associates are tracking phones near abortion clinics. Yours showed up near a handful of facilities."

Phoebe drifted away again, then turned back to me, her forehead creased by a deep furrow. For a moment, I thought she was going to unleash a verbal assault, but then her face softened.

"Is that how they found out about Sheila?"

"State officials tracked her phone. A snitch inside the clinic, who was paid by a group led by Tanya Cobb, also reported her. From what I understand, Tanya was doing what the governor wanted. I'm sorry to be so blunt, but I don't like the governor or any of his cronies."

"So, there are other women who are going to be charged like Sheila? That's what my father is pushing for?"

I nodded. "It appears so."

"Everyone lies to me. Why should I believe you?"

I grabbed my phone. "I'm sending you a memo, the gist of which is that Tanya and the attorney general are carrying out your father's wishes. The memo makes clear he cares more about his political agenda than he does about the health and safety of women. He used Daniel Lockhart to get to Sheila. Now she's dead, but he isn't done. He's planning on bringing charges against other women."

"You're a lawyer. Can't you protect these women? The law should protect them, not punish them."

I pursed my lips. "I'm just a simple prosecutor with no power to do anything. Or at least I was a prosecutor. It's hard to know what my status is. Anyway, in a few months, I'll be out of a job. So, the answer to your question is no, I can't protect them. To put a point on it, I'm trying hard to protect myself and my daughter from the consequences of trying to find justice for Sheila."

Phoebe suddenly closed her eyes and shuddered. I saw her hands shake and her eyes twitching.

"If I'm prying or if this is too stressful—"

She took a deep breath. "This happens occasionally. I've tried to tell the quacks my father hired that the shit they prescribed for me is making it worse. I never heard voices before or found myself in places with no memory of how I got there. Even crack didn't affect me like this. The ticks you see are new, but I can't quit taking the goddamned medication without being sent to a mental health clinic. I've been there a few times, and I'm not going back. Not without a straitjacket. I could use a glass of water, maybe with a straw if you have one."

She sipped the water, then nodded as if agreeing to something. "You're certain Daniel Lockhart raped Sheila?"

"Her and others. I don't know how many. Mind you, I can't prove he raped anyone else, but I'm certain he did."

"And you think my father knows about Mr. Lockhart's past?"

"That's my opinion. Maybe he didn't know at first, but I think he knows now. Certainly, Tanya knows, but it doesn't seem to concern any of them."

She sat silently, staring at me, but I was certain she didn't see me. If it hadn't been for the slight changes at the corners of her mouth, I might have thought she'd gone catatonic.

Suddenly, Phoebe pushed back from the table and stood, her breathing rapid and shallow. "What you're saying," she yelled, jabbing her finger at me, "is that my father and lawyers like Phillip Dunlevy are going to let a rapist go free while people like you persecute rape victims who had abortions? And you can't stop him? No one can stop him? That's what you're saying?"

"Phoebe…"

She closed her eyes and tilted her head back. "Someone has to do something. Someone has to…"

"I didn't mean to… Listen to me."

Phoebe bolted from the kitchen. A moment later, I heard the front door slam.

I sat for a moment considering whether I should have been more diplomatic in the way I answered Phoebe's questions or not answered them at all. Had I upset her unnecessarily?

I waited to be visited by a wave of regret, but whether I was too tired or simply burned out, the feeling never materialized.

CHAPTER TWENTY-FIVE

With the house empty again, I got busy. Dishes were cleaned, beds changed, and carpets vacuumed. I willed myself not to think about anything important and was modestly successful.

Harper had reluctantly agreed to send me a text every hour to confirm she was okay. Her last text was the words, "still alive," a not-too-subtle indication that she found the heartbeat messages irksome.

I settled into drinking wine and watching an awful movie on Netflix. Half a bottle later, an impulse to unclutter the house, to simplify my life, to pretend I was moving overwhelmed me. I started in the kitchen and moved to the bedrooms. I began by sorting old clothes, knickknacks, and photos into piles of tossers, keepers, and undecideds. For nearly an hour, the effort was liberating. Then, a wine headache brought me back to reality.

I had forgotten how many full closets I had and what I had packed in them. The piles grew, and I lost my ability to discern junk from cherished items. What was once on hangers and hung in an orderly fashion was jammed into the bottom of closets to be sorted another day.

The one enduring consequence of this failed effort was that I'd found a box containing my childhood diaries. I sat on the floor and removed the three volumes reverently. The words in these notebooks were those of a person who, though not technically dead, was no longer living. They told the thoughts and aspirations of an innocent girl and her memories, memories colored by naivete that had yet to be corrupted by disappointment, hurt, and betrayal. I yearned to reconnect with that girl but was unsure what I might say to her or her to me. I slipped the diaries back into the box and placed it at the back of my closet. Perhaps another time.

I had an hour before I had to pick up Harper and needed to summon the strength to put on a good face. I set an alarm and lay on the bed, closed my eyes, and drifted into a dreamless slumber.

•   •   •

The buzz of my phone pulled me from my sleep. For a moment, I thought it was my alarm, but it was Eric calling me on my burner phone.

"Has something happened?"

"Maybe. I have a friend in the governor's protection detail. There's been a shooting at the country club where the governor is staying. I don't have the details, but my contact said someone saw the governor's daughter leaving the grounds in a hurry. It's all over the news."

"Phoebe? Oh god…"

I heard a faint ring. "Hang on. Someone's calling on my other phone."

"I'll pick up Harper and come over. We can install your webcams while all this shakes out."

I darted into the kitchen and retrieved the phone from the table without checking the number, managed a quick hello, and waited.

"Mom?" said Harper meekly, her voice wavering. "Mom. I just wanted to come home…"

"Ashley? Daniel here. I—"

"Don't you touch her," I said in a voice I didn't recognize. "Don't you…"

I looked at my other phone, but the call with Eric had been disconnected.

"Shush and listen. Harper is fine and will stay that way, but you have to do what I tell you. The first rule is you don't call anyone. Got that? Keep your phone on so I can hear everything you say. I'm going to text you an address where we can all get together for a chat."

"Please, Daniel. Just let Harper go."

"We need to meet first and discuss how you fucked up my life. In a moment, you'll be able to see with your own eyes."

I scribbled the address on a notepad. "Where is this?"

"It's on the river. You'll find it using maps but be careful not to disconnect the call. I don't trust you."

"I'm leaving now. Just don't hurt her."

"Mom! He doesn't want to chat. He's got a gun."

I heard a scuffle and Harper screaming.

"What are you doing?!"

"She's like her mother. She doesn't know when to keep her mouth shut, so I had to gag her. Get going before I lose patience with both of you."

I turned on the television and quickly lowered the volume. The breaking news was chilling:

"In a shocking development, the governor, his lieutenant governor, and the attorney general have been shot at a country club outside the Village of Freeman's Gate. We have unconfirmed reports of at least one fatality. And if the shooting wasn't shocking enough, police say they are looking for the governor's daughter, Phoebe Adams, as a fourth victim or possibly a person of interest."

"Who are you talking to?!"

"No one. I came into the kitchen and the television was on. I'll turn it off. I'm sorry. I'm leaving my house and getting in my car. The phone will connect through the car radio, so don't be alarmed if there's a change in the way my voice sounds."

"I'm not stupid," snapped Daniel. "Just keep talking."

When I stepped outside, I was greeted by a warm, swirling wind that tormented the tall oaks and filled the air with what remained of last year's leaves. To the west, dark, billowing clouds the color of a bruise filled the horizon. And while the sun was still shining, the air was heavy with the smell of rain. It was as if Mother Nature had conjured up a tempest to dramatize the storm that was raging in my head.

"All right. I'm heading toward the river, but I don't know how to use maps while I'm talking on the phone. I'm not good with technology. Just tell me which way to go."

"When you get to Shilo Road, turn left."

"Okay. Can I talk to Harper?"

"No, you can't. She's as comfortable as I can make her under the circumstances."

"What circumstances? I'm turning left on Shilo."

"Check to see if you're being followed. Take the next right and pull over. Wait a minute and if no one turns, make a U-turn and get back on Shilo Road. In a mile or so, you'll come over a hill. About halfway down the other side, you'll see a driveway marked by a Private-Property-Keep-Out sign. Come to the end of the drive and just walk it. The door isn't locked because the druggies kept breaking it."

I confirmed I wasn't being followed. A few minutes later, I found the driveway and hesitated. I imagined an army of cop cars flying over the hill, with Eric in the lead, coming to Harper's rescue. Daniel would be riddled with bullets, and Harper would escape without a scratch.

But even as the scene played out in my mind, I knew the only way Harper would leave Daniel's clutches alive would be if Eric took him by surprise or if I could distract him long enough for her to run away. Any sign that the police had been called and Harper would be dead.

What Daniel had referred to as a driveway was a rutted, weed-ridden track. My small car bottomed out more than once, and whatever Daniel was saying was drowned out by the sound of weeds and rocks scraping against it.

I came around a curve in the road, and the river came into view. To my right was a partially finished house, its exterior marred by graffiti in an assortment of colors. Some of the art was new, some faded, a testament to how long the house had been neglected. Even in its skeletal state, I saw its potential grandeur making its current condition all the sadder.

Somewhere inside the structure was my daughter and a delusional, desperate man. I had one singular purpose in life: to get her away from him unharmed. How I accomplished this task didn't matter.

As I stepped out of the car, lightning flashed on the horizon. A few seconds later, thunder shattered the quiet and a chilly wind whipped up a cloud of dust. The rain arrived as I climbed a set of temporary stairs, pushed the door open, and stepped inside.

"Nice of you to join us," said Daniel. "And yes, that's a gun pressed into your back. See what you made me become? But I've forgotten my manners. Before we get down to business, I'd like to give you a tour of my dream home, the one you destroyed. We can pretend what it might have looked like before you ruined my life."

He led me to a room with a high ceiling, a massive stone fireplace, and an exterior wall adorned with stately windows. Flashes of lightning filled the room with an eerie blue-white light that offered glimpses of what it could have been.

"Be careful of the needles and excrement." He spun around and pointed the gun at me. "This was going to be my living room, the place where I would spend my days looking at the river and the birds and animals. In the winter, I'd sit by the fireplace over there and read. It's hard to see right now because of the storm, but the natural light that filled this room was exquisite. I don't have any electricity, so we'll have to make do."

He gestured with his free hand. "To be clear, I didn't plan on having holes in the drywall or the word 'fuck' spray painted everywhere. That happened after you charged me with a crime and I had to pay a lawyer and my contractors abandoned me. The glass on the floor over there is from a beautiful antique chandelier. I had it installed just after the workers finished painting the ceiling. Scum bags used it for target practice. Now look at it."

The pounding on the roof intensified, and the lightning came more frequently.

"I want to see Harper."

Daniel sighed and then waved the gun at me. "You could show me just a little fucking respect." He glared at me. "This way."

I tripped on a two-by-four and fell on the floor with a loud grunt.

"Show me your hands," snapped Daniel. After he was satisfied they were empty, I gathered my cell phone and got to my feet. A trickle of blood ran down my leg and then dripped onto the floor.

We entered what I guessed was going to be the kitchen. The walls were framed, and the plumbing roughed in, but the appliances and cabinets were absent. Daniel had tied Harper to a chair and stuffed a towel into her mouth. Next to her was a small wooden chair covered with dried paint of varying colors. Daniel motioned for me to sit on it.

"I had the best appliances and beautiful maple cabinets. When the money dried up, I had to return them, minus a restocking fee and shipping."

He pulled my arms behind me and secured my hands to the arms of the chair with zip ties. A moment later, he pulled the gag from Harper's mouth. She coughed and then looked at me, sobbing.

"I'm sorry, Mom. I shouldn't have left the school, but I just wanted to go home. I didn't think…"

"She didn't think I'd be watching her," said Daniel. "Let's face it. A protective order is just a piece of paper. I'm sure a lot of women whose loved ones beat or kill them have a protective order to wave around. Doesn't help much when the man sucker punches them in the face." He shrugged. "We don't need to go through all that. We have stuff to talk about and decisions to make and not much time."

Daniel reached over and gently touched Harper's cheek. "So young and pretty. I bet you're mean to the ugly kids. You probably sit with the in-crowd during lunch, with the other pretty people."

"I don't," said Harper, pulling her head away. "They don't like me and I don't like them."

"Really?"

I pulled on the zip tie, but it remained taunt and unrelenting. When I looked up, Daniel was standing over me. I saw a blur of the gun barrel as it moved toward my head, then felt the sting of hard metal on my right temple. The blow knocked the chair to the floor, shattering it. I could hear Harper screaming, but her voice was faint and distant.

"Now look what you made me do," said Daniel.

Blood washed over my right eye, but I could still see him hovering. He pointed the automatic at me.

"I was an excellent teacher," he said, his voice cracking. "I was a model citizen. I had a life, a good life. This was going to be my reward. I was cured of the impulses that drove me as a young man, and then that bitch Sheila revived my demons. She deserved what she got. Everything that happened after that was your fault. Now you will have to watch as I take from you what you cherish most. Get up."

I rolled to my knees, but my head was still spinning.

He turned to Harper and tore her blouse from her.

"Mom!"

"No! Not her. Me. Hurt me."

Daniel froze, then burst from the kitchen. As I struggled to clear my head, I heard him mutter, "What the fuck?" A moment later, he returned. He paced and spoke incoherently, and then turned and pointed the gun at Harper's head.

"What's Phillip doing here? Tell me!"

"I don't know! I—"

"I told you not to call anyone. Fuck!".

"I didn't. I didn't call anyone. You were listening. Why would I call Phillip?"

"Daniel?" The familiar voice came from the foyer. "I'm here with Phoebe Adams. She's the governor's daughter. We want to speak to you about a pardon. Can you let us in so we can do that?"

Daniel didn't answer. Phillip and Phoebe appeared, and he eyed them. I was still on my knees and saw the gun in Phoebe's hand partially hidden behind her back. For a moment, the room went black, the inky solitude punctuated by flashes of blue light. I wanted to give in to the darkness, but I willed myself to stay conscious. I watched the others through fluttering eyes and heard voices that sounded unworldly. I couldn't abandon Harper.

I saw Daniel point the gun at Phillip. "You're lying. Why would the governor pardon me? You're trying to trick me."

"No, Daniel," said Phillip, "it's not a trick. Phoebe came to my office with the news. I thought you'd be here. You've been through a lot and maybe it's just been too much, you know. We just want to make all this go away. No one has to get hurt. You can start clean. Maybe we can get you some money to fix your house. Can we talk about that?"

Phoebe glanced at me, then at Harper.

"I'm done talking," he said. The room filled with the crack of the gun and Phillip keeled over. Before he hit the floor, more shots rang out. Phoebe grabbed her side. Daniel seemed stunned, but I could make no sense of it.

Daniel took a step toward Harper. I summoned all my strength. In a moment, I was airborne, an angry mother protecting her young. Daniel saw me and turned to defend himself, but he was too late. He fired again, setting my shoulder on fire. He tumbled backward, slamming his head against the exposed studs. I fell to the floor, unable to move, gripped by the fear that I had failed in my most important moment.

I drifted into a sea of grayness, a state in which I could hear but not see. Harper was crying. Phoebe was trying to comfort her.

Then I heard the words, "Hi, Daniel." The voice that spoke was so soft and lyrical that I thought it could have come from inside my head. I listened as the voice continued.

"You don't know me and you never will. I wanted you to know that I understand you, or at least how demons control you. I don't think I'm controlled by demons, but perhaps angels with attitude. I'm on a quest to rid the world of people who hurt people. My father was one of them, and so were his colleagues. Society takes a dim view of vigilantism, but I think it's what I was born to do. I have never felt such clarity as I do now."

I heard a muffled *pop*. Then my gray world went all black.

EPILOGUE

As a prosecutor, I have often been frustrated by witnesses who, though present for a crime, can't remember anything about it. You'd think they'd know the color of the car or the height of the perp, but not so.

I was, in theory, a witness to the shooting of Phillip Dunlevy and Daniel Lockhart, but despite my best efforts, I have very little recollection of what actually happened. Granted, I was struck in the head and shot. But even though I was conscious for the major events, I only had snippets of memories, many of which conflicted with the evidence gathered at the scene.

With me eliminated as a reliable witness, and Phoebe admitting to being medicated, Harper's description of the events that left Phillip and Daniel dead and Phoebe and me wounded, was what the police deemed to be the most reliable version of events.

Harper related what she saw with confidence, and the investigating detectives used her story as the basis for their report.

While I couldn't remember what happened precisely, the events Harper described left me with the odd feeling that something was off, but of course, I couldn't say how. The police were impressed with how precisely she detailed what transpired, but her certainty made me uneasy.

When I verbalized my concerns to Eric, he dismissed them. "You are a control person. Not remembering the shootings has riddled you with doubt. Harper's story makes sense. It explains everything the forensic team found at the scene. You need to find satisfaction in that the four people who made your life miserable and threatened you and your daughter are dead and that Sheila has found a modicum of justice. You need to heal and move on."

The official account of the shootings at the country club and Daniel's unfinished house offers a plausible explanation of who did what and when.

"March 8:

"At approximately 11:30 AM, Phoebe Adams called on Ashley Corbin at her home. She left approximately thirty minutes later. She was agitated, but did not appear to be violent or contemplating violence.

"At about 12:30 PM, Daniel Lockhart came to the country club outside Freeman's Gate, where Governor Adams, Lieutenant Governor Tanya Cobb, and Attorney General Carl Hinton were staying, and shot them. The governor died at the scene. The other two victims were pronounced dead at the hospital. A fourth person, Phoebe Adams, the governor's daughter, managed to escape. She hid until Daniel left the scene. Concerned for the safety of Ashley Corbin, her daughter, Harper, and Phillip Dunlevy, she drove first to the Corbin residence, and, not finding anyone home, to the office of Mr. Dunlevy.

"While there, Ms. Adams expressed the view from things she overheard at the country club that Daniel may have kidnapped Ashley and/or Harper. At this point, neither Phillip nor Phoebe knew the governor was dead. Phillip concluded that if Daniel had taken either of them, the place he would go was his unfinished home near the river. They agreed that if they found Daniel with Ashley and/or Harper, they would tell Daniel that the governor had offered him a pardon and that all would be forgiven.

"While Phoebe was en route from the country club, Daniel kidnapped Harper Corbin from school, then used the threat of violence to her person to convince Ashley to meet him at a property owned by Mr. Lockhart. Daniel secured both Ashley and Harper to chairs and struck Ashley with the barrel of a gun, knocking her to the floor. The chair she was tied to broke on impact, releasing her hands from the zip ties that had secured them to the chair's arms.

"Phoebe's suspicions were correct. Daniel moved into position to shoot Ashley but was interrupted by the arrival of Phillip and Phoebe. At this point, Daniel, believing Phillip had or was planning to betray him, shot and killed Phillip. Phoebe was wounded by bullet fragments that momentarily immobilized her. Ashley, free of her restraints, then attacked Daniel and drove him into the wall, but not before he shot her in the shoulder.

"At this point, Eric Graham arrived having found Daniel's address written on a notepad at Ashley's house. Seeing Eric, Daniel turned his gun on himself and fired a fatal shot to his heart.

"Because of the storm, the police response to the incident was delayed. Eric, acting on his own, took the wounded to the hospital for treatment."

The timeline had to be reconciled with the forensic data, most of which focused on blood splatter and ballistic analysis. What was indisputable was that the caliber of the gun used to kill the three politicians was the same as that used to kill Phillip Dunlevy. However, the bullet that took his life was never found. The round passed through his eye, out the back of his head, and was inexplicably lost. Blood splatter suggested that the slug should have been buried in the wall behind him, but a thorough search failed to locate it.

The bullet that struck my shoulder was lost as well. The bullet that killed Daniel was recovered and matched the gun that killed Governor Adams, Lieutenant Governor Cobb, and Attorney General Hinton. All told, Daniel had killed five people, including himself.

I couldn't refute the story, but wasn't buying it, especially the part that made Phoebe out to be both a victim and a hero. I was surprised that no one questioned the conclusion that Daniel had committed suicide when he could have shot me or Harper and let Eric shoot him. To be fair, I don't recall Eric's arrival, so I can't dispute the official version of the story, but I wasn't believing it either.

What no one could explain was my recollection that I saw a gun tucked into the back of Phoebe's jeans. Only one gun was found in Daniel's house and that was the murder weapon. My memory of a second gun was explained away as a product of wishful thinking (meaning I imagined it) because I wanted someone to save Harper from Daniel. It was also suggested that because I was suffering from a severe concussion, I wasn't in my right mind.

They also dismissed the words I heard Phoebe speak to Daniel as fantasy, a projection of what I might have said if I'd had a gun and could have shot him. Whatever I remembered that contradicted the official story was explained away as the hallucinations of a woman with a brain injury.

Two aspects of the official account concerned me. First, the narrative portrayed Phoebe as a rational young woman capable of thinking logically. But hours before the shooting at the country club, she sat in my kitchen, barely able to maintain an intelligent conversation.

The other hole in the official account was the alleged offer by the governor to pardon Daniel. Assuming that Daniel shot the governor, he would have known immediately that the offer was a lie. Yet, he expressed puzzlement, not disbelief. This discrepancy was explained away as a misunderstanding on my part of his reaction (puzzlement and disbelief were easily confused) and that the reason Daniel shot Phillip was that he knew the pardon offer was a lie. The lie simply reinforced Daniel's belief that Phillip had betrayed him.

I had an alternative theory that explained the chain of events and my so-called hallucinations. The centerpiece of my theory was that Phoebe shot Daniel with the mysterious second gun. Given that the ballistics identified the bullet that killed Daniel came from the same gun that killed the three victims at the country club, it followed that Phoebe was also the shooter at that venue and had killed her father. Under this theory, Phillip and I were shot with Daniel's weapon. Phoebe or someone, most likely Eric, then disposed of Daniel's gun and the evidence that proved its existence. The voice I heard telling Daniel he was about to die was Phoebe's.

One other implication of my two-gun theory was that my conversation with Phoebe that preceded the country club shootings had incited her to murder. That made me an accessory to the murder of the governor and his colleagues, if not legally then morally. Perhaps this was one reason I kept the theory to myself. I also owed Phoebe my life and Harper's and was smart enough to realize that if people I trusted, like Eric and Harper, accepted a set of alternate facts, they must have had good reasons, even if I wasn't privy to them.

The story as Harper told it was accepted, and that's what mattered. If she were keeping some big secret, who was I to complain? That Phoebe may have gotten away with murder was a detail to be weighed against the good that ensued from killing her father and the others.

To be clear, despite my doubts about how the shootings unfolded, I'm not unhappy with the outcome. The long-term consequences of the murders will take time to sort out. Whether the political environment will change for the better or get even more combative is anyone's guess. While I don't normally wish people dead, I don't mourn the passing of the governor and his associates or Daniel Lockhart. Phillip, as Martin would say, was collateral damage. I'm sure there were people saddened by their deaths, but I wasn't one of them.

What haunted me at night wasn't the killings per se, but whether anything would change because of them. A power vacuum in a political institution was like a black hole that sucked in all the best and worst human instincts with equal voracity. Some voices could be heard advocating for change, for a return to what was termed "civilized discourse," but I had my doubts about whether anyone was listening. Cynically, I even doubted that the advocates were sincere and were merely cloaking themselves in words that sounded rational as a wolf on his way to Grandma's house might wear a sheepskin.

Elections were six months away. Whether voters had learned anything from the death of Sheila Fanning remained to be seen.

My shoulder injury was quick to heal, but not my head. I experienced debilitating headaches that required powerful painkillers. The medication enhanced the fog that dulled my thoughts and left me emotional. Martin placed me on administrative leave with full pay and told me not to come back to work until I was fully recovered.

In the days immediately following the shootings, I couldn't take care of myself, much less help Harper deal with the trauma of being abducted and witnessing the murders of two people. Fortunately, I didn't have to. Helena arrived shortly after the shootings and, together with Eric and Liz, cared for both Harper and me. When I could travel, Eric took us to Helena's alpaca ranch, where Harper could attend class remotely.

To my surprise, both a physical therapist and a crisis psychotherapist offered services in Sumner two days a week. Helena related that the crisis doctor had come to Sumner after a school shooting and was still treating parents and students years later. I was relieved that Harper took to her.

Besides our doctor visits, we took walks and enjoyed the companionship of cats, dogs, a goat, and alpacas of all dispositions, and Helena's nurturing. Ranch-life agreed with us. Life was getting better.

We had planned to stay with Helena for a few weeks, but our departure date continued to roll into the future. Nothing was compelling us to return to Freeman's Gate, and we had lots of reasons to stay on the ranch. But in late May, Harper signaled she was ready to return to school, her friends, and her home. I, too, was ready to move on, even as I was unsure what that might mean.

Curiously, her therapist asked if we had any pets at home. She noted that Harper's recovery had dramatically improved when she took responsibility for caring for the animals on the ranch, particularly the mother cat and her litter of kittens. Even Helena pitched the idea of fostering a cat or two on our return to Freeman's Gate. I was suspicious about the origin of the idea but agreed on the condition that the felines could stay with us until we could find permanent homes.

A few days after settling into our old life, we brought Blakely, the orange tabby with PTSD, and a gray cat named Rascal, into our lives. The kitties' sponsor and veterinarian, Terry Logan, offered to help in the transition and address any issues that might arise. Harper was always finding "issues" and reasons why a consultation with Terry was needed. What she didn't seem to grasp is that over time, his visits had less and less to do with the cats. Blakely is now a lap cat who likes his belly rubbed. Rascal lives up to his name and although sweet and affectionate, seems to believe that anything on a counter belongs on the floor.

The felines deserve credit for improving our lives. It's still too early to know just how much.

While there's no silver lining to a heinous crime, I was pleased that shortly after the murder of her father, Phoebe voluntarily committed herself to a psychiatric clinic. A few days after returning home, I received a text inviting me to visit her. I pondered the request, particularly her motivation. I had no interest in revisiting old wounds or trying to find answers to satisfy my lingering doubts about what happened on the day of the shooting. I was, however, curious to see how Phoebe was coping and why she'd reached out to me. After some hesitation, I accepted.

Waiting in the visitor's lounge, I was inexplicably nervous about the visit. I imagined her being escorted by men in white coats, her arms secured in a straitjacket. But when I saw the young woman coming towards me, all my doubts evaporated. Gone were the piercings and vacant eyes. I was gifted a look of joy, and, before I could speak, a crushing embrace.

"Look at you!" I said approvingly.

She laughed. "The crazy house suits me. Sorry, that was the old me. The doctors here have helped me see things as they are, to take responsibility, and deal with guilt constructively."

For a moment, the joy drained from her eyes, only to return as quickly as it departed. "Anyway, let's take a walk and talk about things other than me. I want to hear about Harper and how you're feeling. If you have questions, I'll answer them."

The grounds of the clinic were beautifully landscaped. Benches and chairs had been placed where patients could sit and visit with guests or be alone, if that's what suited them. We strolled along a small pond and chatted about Harper, Phoebe's plans, my plans, and everything but the event that cemented our lives together.

"You must wonder," she said softly, "about what I did when I left your house."

I turned and faced her.

"What you did was bring your world, and mine, back into balance, back to equilibrium. The details don't matter."

She touched my cheeks, then pressed her forehead against mine.

"Equilibrium. I like that. I like that a lot."

Indeed.

ABOUT THE AUTHOR

Light attended both engineering and law school (apparently, unable to make up his mind). He spent three decades practicing law, including environmental, energy, contract, telecommunications, and patent law. (Do you see a pattern here?) But he yearned to be a teller of stories that both entertain and enlighten and published his first novel in 2002. *The Last Rights* will be his sixth published novel. When he's not traveling with his spouse, Sonya, or not writing, he is a dedicated servant to their cat, Feste. He enjoys trying Asian-inspired recipes, experimenting with his air fryer (you don't need one but it really is fun), and reading about new energy technologies (super-hot geothermal looks promising). So much to dabble in. So little time.

NOTE FROM ELLIOTT LIGHT

Word-of-mouth is crucial for any author to succeed. If you enjoyed *The Last Rights*, please leave a review online—anywhere you are able. Even if it's just a sentence or two. It would make all the difference and would be very much appreciated.

Thanks!
Elliott Light

We hope you enjoyed reading this title from:

www.blackrosewriting.com

Subscribe to our mailing list – *The Rosevine* – and receive **FREE** books, daily deals, and stay current with news about upcoming releases and our hottest authors. Scan the QR code below to sign up.

Already a subscriber? Please accept a sincere thank you for being a fan of Black Rose Writing authors.

View other Black Rose Writing titles at www.blackrosewriting.com/books and use promo code **PRINT** to receive a **20% discount** when purchasing.